Making Sense of the
Writer's Workshop

Table of Contents

"I seek words. I chase after them.
When I write, I'm trying to put the most
beautiful words in the world down on paper."

-Cynthia Rylant

Introduction

What an experience it was to watch a talented PreK teacher on the first day of school! She had large pieces of various colors of paper on the floor and different sizes, types, and colors of writing tools available for her students as they walked in the door. She invited them to write whatever they wanted to write about. The students were ready to dive in and there was no separation anxiety for the parents. It was obvious from the beginning that the students viewed themselves as writers, and that the teacher believed in them as writers.

There were many times when my (Patty's) second graders were disappointed because our day was getting short and we still hadn't gotten to Writer's Workshop. I heard remarks like, "But I need to finish editing with Kaitlyn!" and "My first draft is almost ready to be read for revision." Writing was important to them. It was as if their day was incomplete if they didn't write.

Many times we have asked ourselves the questions, "What happens to a student's confidence in themselves as writers? Why do they groan in later years instead of rushing to pick up the pen when writing is mentioned?" When I (Barbara) was teaching Grade 5 in a school that promoted writing to prompts, I was met with a chorus of groans when I even mentioned the word "write." How very enlightening when the following year in a different school the same age group was thrilled because it was finally time to write. The only obvious difference was that these students had participated in Writer's Workshop from the very beginning of their school experience. Their teachers had instilled within them the value of writing. Their love of writing had been nurtured and allowed to grow.

When instruction focuses only on the test-taking skills of writing, using prompts, and prescriptive writing, the result is often the creation of students who dislike writing. They tend to produce only the minimum that is required, often without the quality and individuality of the writer's voice.

It is vital that teachers see themselves as writers, mentors, and guides, supporting students' writing development in a risk-free atmosphere of collaboration. Teachers who build on students' strengths by modeling and gradually releasing the writing process to students, foster the development of skilled, independent writers who perceive themselves as authors. Student choice plays a motivational role in the quality of writing that a student produces. We want students to be excited about writing and to know that writing is an essential part of their lives! The love of writing helps students become better writers. Better writers usually become better readers and more successful test-takers.

In this book, we will explore why the Writer's Workshop model is beneficial to students and teachers, the implementation of Writer's Workshop in the classroom, and ways to support students as they progress as writers.

Chapter 1: **What Is Writer's Workshop?**

Writer's Workshop is a daily, scheduled block of time in which students are provided opportunities to write. Fountas and Pinnell (2001) define Writer's Workshop as "an interrelated combination of writing experiences that occur during the writing block of language/literacy framework. It encompasses focused writing—both assigned and self selected—in a variety of genres and content areas, including longer research projects."

The purpose of Writer's Workshop is to create efficient and effective student writers, each one with a distinct voice and style. In addition, students will develop vocabulary knowledge in an authentic way, while gaining confidence in themselves as writers. Students learn to value the writing process and understand the benefits of being able to express their thoughts in writing.

To develop any new skill, students must receive quality instruction and modeling, attend to think-alouds, repeatedly practice in authentic contexts, receive feedback, and be motivated to perfect their work. Before Writer's Workshop was widely accepted, teachers assigned a writing task, the student completed it, and the teachers graded students' work. Assigning a task, however, does not equal teaching. Writer's Workshop is the context in which the teaching takes place.

Let's imagine for a moment what we would see if we walk into a classroom where a Writer's Workshop is taking place. It is immediately evident that this classroom is filled with students who love to write. It's easy to be in awe at the amount of writing students do! We would expect to see students writing, but the surprise may be the quiet buzz that indicates that there are authors at work. Some are reading and talking about their writing with peers—heads together and engaged in conversations filled with purpose and "writer's talk." Students are busy offering suggestions, comments, and support to one another about word usage, literary elements, or story development. Some students are writing independently on drafts, while others are busy rereading, revising, editing, and publishing their piece of writing in a peer conference. The teacher is moving quietly around the room conferencing with students, yet not interrupting the atmosphere of writers collaborating and working independently.

The walls are filled with anchor posters giving students resources from which to become a more complete, complex writer, indicating that writing is not accidental, but taught with intent. Students may be using the word wall as a resource to choose the word that best fits his or her sentence or check the spelling of a word that doesn't "look right." A sense of confidence is apparent among the students as they work individually, in pairs, or with a small group, writing, editing or revising their drafts. Each student exhibits a feeling of accomplishment when the piece they are writing is completed. There is a feeling of purpose that permeates the room showing the dedication that the students have to their writing. The students seem to know that writing is important business.

We can hear your thoughts now! All of this! This is so complicated. Some teachers believe that Writer's Workshop is overly simplistic and predicable. Others think it too complicated for their teaching style. The truth is, Writer's Workshop is both simple and complex. The Workshop's format is simple. The same three steps are followed daily at approximately the same time in the daily routine.

1. **Mini-Lesson**—During the fifteen minutes of Workshop designated to the mini-lesson, students receive a small dose of extremely important direct teaching. These lessons are short, direct, laser-focused, and based on the needs of the students. Sometimes the lesson's focus is on the operation of the Workshop (procedural mini-lesson), sometimes it's on helping students improve the ways they choose words and arrange them on the page (craft mini-lesson), and at other times the lesson centers on spelling and punctuation or on ways to help readers better understand the writer's intended meaning (convention mini-lessons). Very different in nature, each type of mini-lesson is crucial to the success of the Workshop.

2. **Writing Time**—The writing time is the time students are given to write independently and progress through the writing process at their own pace.

3. **Sharing Time**—This is a time when students have the opportunity to share their writing with the whole class. The teacher sometimes chooses three or four students who have successfully used a skill or writing strategy taught in a mini-lesson.

The Writer's Workshop schedule includes all of these components every day.

Suggested Time Frame for Writer's Workshop

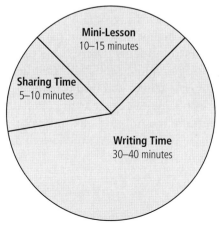

Mini-Lesson
10–15 minutes

Sharing Time
5–10 minutes

Writing Time
30–40 minutes

Mini-Lesson

The mini-lesson is an opportunity for the teacher to suggest skills or strategies that will improve the students' writing. It is also a time to maximize students' participation in the Workshop process. The mini-lesson generally lasts approximately 10–15 minutes. It is taught in a whole-group setting and includes teaching or reteaching a procedure, a strategy for developing or improving a point of the writer's craft, or a convention or skill to improve a student's writing clarity. In order to develop effective mini-lessons, it is vital that the teacher is diligent in observing instructional needs of the students.

Procedural mini-lessons are the student's introduction to the Writer's Workshop. These lessons assure that the Workshop runs smoothly and efficiently, and that students are aware of procedures and expectations. These are often revisited throughout the year as students need to be reminded of the daily operation of the Workshop. These lessons often include anchor charts for students to reference as they become acquainted with Writer's Workshop routines. If the student has not had experience with Writer's Workshop, be sure to allow sufficient time for students to become familiar and comfortable with the Workshop format and expectations. A few procedural mini-lessons topics are:

- Where and how to sit during whole-group meeting time
- How to listen and participate during whole-group meeting time
- Introduce concept and purpose of Writer's Workshop
- Rules for Writer's Workshop
- Where writers sit during Writer's Workshop
- Location of materials and resources and how they are used
- Silent Writing
- Choosing a topic
- Getting started—I've chosen a topic, now what?
- Introduce the writing process
- Sharing or debriefing writing

See pages 73–177 for suggested procedural mini-lesson plans.

Writing Time

The more time students can devote to practicing their craft, the better writers they will become. The first part of writing time is a stage of silent writing. We suggest at least 15 minutes, but the teacher needs to adjust that time according to the age and developmental needs of the students. During this time it is important for the teacher to model a love of writing and to establish himself/herself as a writer and mentor for the students. Many times teachers will find it helpful to play soothing music to help ensure an atmosphere of calm and quiet as the students write. This is the time for students to either continue the drafting of a piece of writing in progress or begin a new piece. In order to be consistent with the length of silent writing time, it may be helpful for the teacher to set a timer.

After the timer sounds, the students have options. They are free to continue writing with their silent writing task, or to resume the writing process with a previously completed draft. During this time, students may be engaged in writing or they may be at various stages of the writing process: prewriting, drafting, revising, rereading, editing, conferring, or publishing. The teacher used this time to confer with individual students or with groups of writers who have similar needs. Students should write every day for about 20–30 minutes.

Sharing Time

During sharing time, students read their writing in small or whole groups to receive feedback and constructive suggestions from readers and listeners for improvement of writing. A teacher may also invite a student who has attempted to incorporate a skill, strategy, or convention in their writing that was taught during the mini-lesson to share their efforts with the whole group. When a student completes the publishing process he or she may use this time to share the published piece with classmates. The teacher may choose to designate an author's chair for such special occasions. Sharing time is usually the last 5–10 minutes of the Writer's Workshop.

Because Writer's Workshop is true differentiated instruction, it requires planning and a deep knowledge of each student's strengths and weaknesses in order to maximize individual growth. The teacher's role includes:

- Plan whole-group instructions for the daily mini-lesson based on students' needs.

- Give the students the opportunity to write independently.

- Conduct one-on-one conferences with the students based on the needs demonstrated in their writing.

- Provide feedback on a regular basis.

- Plan for students to receive feedback in the form of peer sharing and in response to published works.

As students experience the satisfaction of writing what others are interested in reading, their motivation increases.

Additional Mini-Lesson Suggestions

Procedural Mini-Lessons

- Structuring and sequencing, writing while conferring, and sharing
- Using materials, such as a stapler, staple remover, or hole punch
- Using a Writer's Notebook or writing portfolio
- Writing a heading
- Writing only on one side of the paper so that revision is easier
- What to do if you can't choose a topic
- What to do if you don't know how to spell a word
- How to work in ways which are respectful to other writers
- How to conduct a peer conference
- How to provide appropriate feedback
- How to use the revision checklist
- How to use the editing checklist
- Options for publishing
- Illustrating a published book

Craft Mini-Lessons

- Noticing the world through sketching, list-making, and note-taking
- Getting beyond "I like" and "I love" stories
- Writing based on one interesting idea rather than several less significant ones
- Choosing topics
- Telling life stories that others can relate to
- Writing in a variety of genres
- Writing for a variety of audiences
- "Showing" rather than "telling"
- Describing people
- Omitting unnecessary words, such as **and**, **then**, or **very**
- Writing with voice
- Writing effective leads
- Writing effective endings
- Connecting a lead and an ending
- Writing effective titles
- Adding information to improve clarity
- Deleting information for clarity and conciseness
- Enhancing meaning through illustrations

Convention Mini-Lessons

- Managing space on the page
- Using left-to-right and top-to-bottom progression
- Inserting spaces between words
- Using capital letters to start sentences
- Using periods to end sentences
- Differentiating between complete and incomplete sentences
- Using capital letters for proper nouns
- Using exclamation points
- Using question marks
- Inserting quotation marks
- Using commas to separate items in a series
- Using **-ing** endings
- Using **-ed** endings
- Using contractions
- Spelling (according to grade level)
- Parts of a letter
- Punctuating a letter
- Using picture dictionaries

Chapter 2:
Why Teach Using a Writer's Workshop Model?

As we know, three important aspects of teaching children to write effectively are:

- **Student Choice**—Allowing students to make decisions about writing on topics based on their interests, knowledge about the topic, the connections they can make with the topic, or a topic they want to learn more about.

- **Time to write**—Allowing students the time to effectively plan, record their thoughts, edit, revise, and publish their writing.

- **Constructive feedback**—Allowing students to confer with peers and adults and incorporating the authentic responses to gain information that will help them improve as a writer.

An effective Writer's Workshop incorporates these three elements (Atwell, 1987; Graves, 1983; Routman, 1994; Wood and Dickenson, 2000).

Although some teachers experience frustrations with Writer's Workshop (too time-intensive and too much opportunity for off-task behavior), the advantages far outweigh the disadvantages. The main advantage is that students develop skills and strategies that help them progress along the path toward becoming confident, lifelong writers! Fountas and Pinnell tell us that Writer's Workshop provides the support that students need to become effective writers. Among the many additional benefits of Writer's Workshop are:

Reciprocal Qualities of Reading and Writing

The reading/writing connection is a powerful one: more reading leads to greater writer competency (Stotsky, 1983; Amiran and Mann, 1982; Sudol and Sudol, 1995; Duke and Bennet-Armistead, 2003). Reading and writing are interdependent processes that are essential to each other and mutually beneficial (Holt and Vacca, 1984). As writing improves through daily communicative use, reading is enhanced (Goodman and Goodman, 1983). The relationship between reading and writing is based on communication. Both processes should develop as a natural extension of the child's need to communicate (Wilson, 1981). For most people, it is easier to read the words of others than to write original thoughts. Wide reading, however, provides students with tools to put their original thoughts into words.

Independent Learners

The objective of any teacher should be to promote independence. Because Writer's Workshop is centered around a routine that provides structure as well as choice, students must learn to become self-sufficient within that structure. In fact, the best Workshop teachers value structure and organization (Grave, 1992). Students learn ways to solve problems and meet their needs within the structure of the Workshop.

> "Research is crystal clear: Schools that do well insist that their students write every day and that teachers provide regular and timely feedback."
>
> –Regie Routman

Students learn to utilize necessary materials without constant supervision and to make decisions about their own writing, working independently or within a small group that will provide support for their individual needs.

Differentiated Instruction

During Writer's Workshop the teacher has many opportunities for differentiation during the mini-lesson, during the writing time, and during the sharing time. For example, during student/teacher conferences, the teacher determines one or two instructional points that are specific and unique to that student's writing in order to maximize each student's growth.

Student-Centered Instruction

In the traditional approach to writing instruction, much class time is spent with the teacher lecturing and the students listening and observing. The students then work alone on writing assignments, and cooperation and sharing are not encouraged. In student-centered teaching methods, the focus shifts from the teacher to the learners. Students are engaged in active learning by solving problems, answering questions, and posing questions of their own. They may also discuss, confer, explain, debate, or brainstorm. Students may work individually, with partners, or in small groups to provide positive support. Student-centered instruction, such as Writer's Workshop, has been shown to be superior to the traditional teacher-centered approach to instruction (R.M. Felder and R. Brent, 2009).

Lifelong Learners

Many adults feel comfortable describing themselves as readers, but they do not believe they are writers (Fountas and Pinnell, 2001). Writer's Workshop prepares students to be lifelong writers by providing a forum for expressing themselves authentically in writing. It brings out the writer's voice and shows the importance of being able to express oneself on paper. Through daily instruction and writing practice, students become fluent and competent writers by learning to write in different formats, in different genres, for different purposes, and for different audiences.

When a person is persuaded that something works, it's because you've seen it work. We'd like to share a story with you. We were working in a traditionally low-performing school where a group of excellent Kindergarten teachers were concerned about the lack of direction in their writing instruction. They decided to approach the principal of their school with the idea of shifting their writing instruction to the Writer's Workshop method. After the principal was finally convinced, the teachers began to research and to incorporate Writer's Workshop into every Kindergarten classroom. The teachers immediately saw the value in being able to differentiate writing instruction. They also noticed rapid growth in their students' writing skills, and Writer's Workshop was becoming the students' favorite part of the day! The teachers were so excited! They shared their students' writing success with the Grade 1 teachers. The Grade 1 teachers decided to make the change to the Workshop approach as the kindergartners became first graders. Grade 1 experienced another successful year of writing growth! The following year, the Grade 2 teachers jumped on board. By

> "Differentiated Instruction is a flexible approach to teaching in which the teacher plans and carries out varied approaches to content, process, and product in anticipation of and in response to student differences in readiness, interests, and learning needs."
>
> *–Tomlinson, 1995*

> "If through your workshop they (students) come to believe in themselves as writers, you have given them a gift that will sustain them for years to come."
>
> *–Fletcher and Portalupi, 2001*

the time the students reached Grade 3, the entire school was very aware of the success the primary students had experienced with Writer's Workshop. So, the Grade 3 teachers were happy to give it a try. Now for the exciting part! When this group of students completed the state test in the spring of the Grade 3 year, the results were amazing. The students had the highest Grade 3 writing scores in the district, and the school had reached exemplary status. The teachers will tell you that Writer's Workshop was the key to the students' success.

Chapter 3: **Developmental Stages of Writing**

Writers generally move through many developmental stages as they learn to write. Understanding the developmental stages enables teachers to select appropriate materials and methods to support all writers.

Stages of Writing Development

Scribble Stage: A student operating in the scribble stage writes with lines, scribbles, or mock-letter forms. He or she has no specific concept of the use of space on the page.

Isolated Letter Stage: During the isolated letter stage, letter forms begin to appear. Random letters and numbers recur throughout the writing sample, based on the student's developing knowledge. The student is still confused about such early concepts as words, directionality, and the use of space.

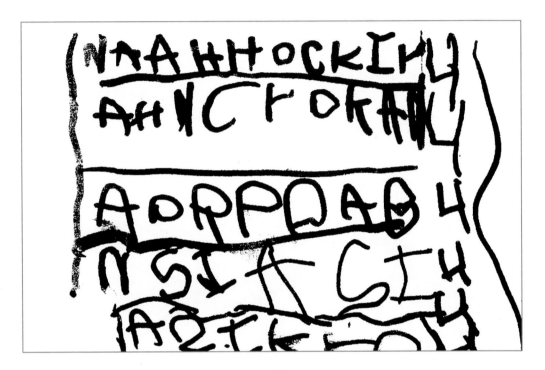

Transitional Stage: Some letter-sound correspondences and correctly spelled words begin to appear as the student moves into the transitional stage. However, they may be mixed with isolated letters and numerals.

Stylized Sentence Stage: As a student acquires a core writing vocabulary of frequently used words, he or she begins to use these words to construct sentences with simple patterns. The student is also beginning to refine concepts of spacing and letter-sound correspondence.

Writing Stage: A student moves beyond the stylized sentence stage as he or she learns to compose stories and acquires a larger writing vocabulary. The student uses more conventional spelling, longer sentences, and punctuation.

Fluent Writers

Fluent writers begin to develop strategies for the craft of writing. These strategies include elaborating (voice), critiquing their own writing and others' writing, writing in different genres, using what they know about reading text to write, using the writing process, and developing a sense of audience. Fluent writers spell most words correctly and carefully edit their spelling while they write. They also have a wide vocabulary and know how to use a thesaurus and dictionary to expand their current vocabulary. Fluent writers understand text structures (compare and contrast, descriptive, procedural, problem/solution, and cause/effect), text functions (narrative, expressive, informative, and poetic), and tenses. They write on a wide variety of topics including personal experiences and nonfiction topics.

Fluent writers:

- Compose text using various genres according to purpose and audience
- Demonstrate success in conforming to expository text structures in informational writing (descriptive, problem/solution, time/order, compare/contrast, cause/effect, and procedural)
- Write independently for self and others
- Incorporate descriptive language into writing
- Gather information on a topic, sort it into categories, and use categories to write paragraphs
- Use graphic organizers to plan and organize writing independently
- Revise writing for content and clarity
- Edit writing for spelling
- Edit writing for correct use of capitalization, punctuation, and proper nouns
- Edit writing for standard grammar usage and subject/verb agreement
- Develop a writer's "voice"
- Write for different audiences
- Use resources including dictionaries, thesaurus, spell-check, and other text references
- Apply knowledge of Writer's Craft from the texts they have read to original writing
- Develop a topic and extend over many pages

During the fluent stage, writers are beginning to exhibit control of a variety of text structures and genres. This student wrote a nonfiction historical piece (see the following page) in descriptive and sequence text structures. Sequence of events flows from one event to the other through the use of transitional indicators, such as dates, times, and words (**began**, **when**, **finally**, **later**). Because this piece is so well organized, it is evident that the writer spent a great deal of time prewriting, revising, and editing his piece.

Strong descriptive words and phrases are used, such as **heart-wrenching, senseless, unthinkable, horrendous**, and **lost forever**. By using this type of elaboration and voice, the reader can visualize the young author's words. Think about this sentence: "The quiet night was shattered by the horrendous sound of ripping and scraping." This sentence creates a visual image in the reader's mind about what the people on board may have been feeling before the event. The word **souls** used in the first paragraph gives honor to the individual people on board. Each person is real when the word **soul** is used. Another good use of voice is the definition of hypothermia. The young writer incorporates many of the writing craft techniques previously modeled and demonstrated by the teacher. Spelling and punctuation are used appropriately and consistently.

Conferencing with the student on specific issues, such as how to develop his or her individual process as a writer and revise to meet his or her purpose and audience, will help the student master the craft of writing.

The Titanic

The sinking of the Titanic was one of the most heart-wrenching events of the 20th century because of the number of lives lost to a senseless accident. After leaving the harbor in Southampton, England on April 10, 1912, the cruise liner sailed for five uneventful days. Some 2,200 souls were on board including some of the richest people in the world.

On April 14 at 11:40pm, the unthinkable happened. The quiet night was shattered by the horrendous sound of ripping and scraping. The Titanic had collided with an iceberg. Water began filling the ship's compartments at all levels, and the ship began to sink. The captain knew another ocean liner, the Carpathia, was also in the North Atlantic and distress calls were sent out. Diligent crew members began the evacuation process only to find that there were not nearly enough lifeboats for all the passengers. When this information spread to passengers, many of them panicked and jumped overboard into the frigid, icy waters of the North Atlantic. Some managed to get into the lifeboats which had been lowered, but most of them drowned or died of hypothermia, a possibly deadly condition which occurs when the body has been exposed to extreme cold. Finally, at approximately 2:20am the Titanic split in two and, after two hours, completely sank to the bottom of the North Atlantic Ocean. The Carpathia located about 700 survivors; all others, some 1,500 people, were lost forever. Many people felt, and still feel, that the captain, Edward J. Smith, was responsible for the accident. Whether this is true or not, Captain Smith chose to go down with his ship. The president of the company that owned the Titanic chose to escape in a lifeboat.

Later, it was discovered that other ships had sent out warnings of icebergs and had traveled further south to avoid them. Somehow, the crew of the Titanic did not hear or heed those warnings.

Today, the Titanic still sits in its watery grave marked only by a plaque placed there by the person who discovered it, Dr. Robert Ballard. Hopefully, it has found a resting place.

Chapter 4: **Classroom Environment**

A well-organized classroom and a well-planned lesson are important in ensuring students' success. There are many factors to consider when organizing the classroom for a successful Writer's Workshop.

1. Classroom Arrangement

A Writer's Workshop classroom should include the following:

- An area where the entire class can gather
- A small-group instruction area
- Independent writing areas
- Storage bins for writing materials and resource books
- Storage areas for equipment, such as computers and tape recorders
- Display areas for interactive charts
- Word walls

Below is a diagram of a possible classroom arrangement.

Room Arrangement for Writer's Workshop

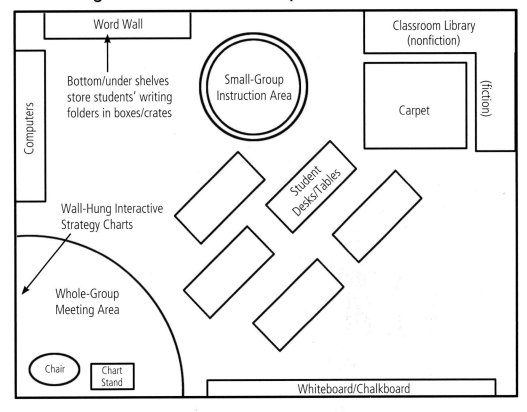

2. Materials

Although each student will require materials specific to his individual development during Writer's Workshop, pens, pencils, markers, paper (lined, blank, and colored), computers, dictionaries, a thesaurus, and basic publishing supplies should be available to all. Below is a list of suggested Workshop materials for students and teachers. Teachers may supply or ask parents to purchase the materials needed by students.

Writer's Workshop Materials

Materials for Students:

- One folder with two pockets (to hold current writing projects, resources, and record sheets)
- One file folder (to hold completed writing work)
- Writer's Notebook
- Container to hold writing materials

Materials for the Teacher:

- Two file boxes—one for storing collected whole-class work; the other for lesson plans, teaching materials, and assessment data
- Record-keeping forms and charts, such as the Status of the Class chart (see sample on page 21)
- Loose-leaf notebook
- File folders

Recording the Status of the Class

Because students work in different stages during Writer's Workshop, teachers may find it helpful to use the six-column Status of the Class chart to record and monitor each student's progress. In the first column, the teacher writes the name of each student. The next five columns are named for the days of the week and contain information regarding where each student is in the writing process (see sample below).

Sample Status of the Class Chart

Student	Monday 5-1	Tuesday 5-2	Wednesday 5-3	Thursday 5-4	Friday 5-5
Mary	Pre-Write	Draft	Draft	Draft	Revise
Juan	Revise	Absent	Revise	Edit	Publish

Teachers may keep the Status of the Class charts in the teacher's notebook, a clipboard, or on a chart on a wall. The purpose is for the teacher to be able to support the students in their efforts to progress through the writing process.

Atmosphere

An atmosphere of collaboration, teamwork, and respect is essential for a successful Writer's Workshop. Writer's Workshop must take place in a risk-free environment where students are supported and feel comfortable expressing their thoughts orally and in writing. The belief that writers are valued and that authentic writing is an important part of each day can be felt throughout the room. The students may feel comfortable to seek that special place where they love to write—like a quiet corner, a comfortable chair, or at a table. As the teacher, we need to bring those considerations into our classroom and design the arrangement of our room with the different requirements of all of our students in mind.

Along with carving out spaces for individuals, and whole-group and small-group meetings within our classroom, special attention must also be given to the walls of a classroom because they tell a story. What evidence of learning about authentic writing do others see as they walk into the room? Do they notice that the teacher and the students value writing? Do the students always write on assigned topics, or are they given a choice? What can be observed about the students' learning simply by "reading" the wall? The walls are the teacher's and writer's stage for displaying their craft!

When students have a comfortable space, time to write, and an atmosphere of acceptance and collaboration, students will take the risk to express their thoughts on paper. If you build it, they will write.

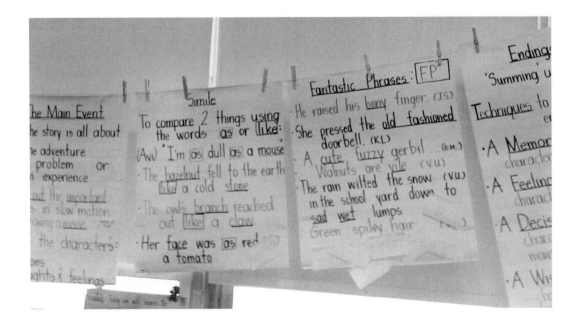

Chapter 5:
How Does a Teacher Establish Routines and Procedures?

We were visiting a school where Writer's Workshop was a regular part of the day for most students. When we walked into the classroom, we were greeted by a student who was a designated host. The teacher joined us and in the process of welcoming us to her room, she introduced the student as the host for the day. The student's responsibility was to escort visitors around their room, showing and explaining how the class functioned during Writer's Workshop. She was able to explain in detail how the Workshop operated in this classroom. We were thrilled! Not only did this student understand the steps of the writing process, but she was able to clearly explain to us how the classroom was organized, and how the students moved quietly about in the room as they proceeded through the writing cycle. This classroom was dedicated to the idea that all of these students were writers. It was student-centered instruction in a very organized and concise way with no doubt about the purpose or how to achieve this purpose. We were shown where the writing folders were stored, where the writing table with paper, pencils, editing materials, resources, and tools for publishing was located and the rules for using these supplies. We were shown the area of the room where students met with a peer or an adult when they were ready to have their writing edited. We were invited to observe a response group where students were working together helping an author revise his work. The host was proud to show us the classroom library where there was a special section devoted to student writing so that classmates could share in the enjoyment of reading the published works of their peers. What an informative experience we had!

After the classroom tour, we had a chance to visit with the teacher. We only had one question: How?! Her response was, "I devote the first six weeks of school to establishing the procedures that I want students to use for the rest of the year. If I want students to know how to act, what to do, and their purpose as learners in my room, I have to show them specifically what to do and how to do it. I find that there are times when it is necessary to revisit some of our procedures and reteach using mini-lessons throughout the year. Any of my students could have been the host today. That job is not assigned; it's simply the 'luck of the draw.'"

The success of Writer's Workshop depends primarily upon the students' understanding of procedures and routines. Only when students learn to be responsible, respectful, and orderly, can learning take place. It is extremely important that in the early days of Writer's Workshop teachers devote numerous mini-lessons to procedures and routines. (See pages 73–177 for procedural mini-lessons.) Once habits are well established, teachers must continue to reinforce them, as well as teach new ones as the year progresses.

One thing that helps assure a well-run Workshop is the understanding that everyone involved has clear roles and responsibilities. For example, the teacher's role is to plan, model, and reinforce new writing strategies, skills, and behaviors that will take students through the various stages of writing development. The teacher makes authentic, meaningful writing a priority. The teacher becomes a mentor to the students by sharing his or her own writing. The writing can be used as a model for some of the strategies, skills, and conventions being taught. The teacher's professional responsibility also includes explicit, effective instruction that is determined by frequent ongoing assessment of student's work and is based on the requirements of district and state grade-level standards.

Teacher's responsibilities also include making decisions about the practical aspects of running a Writer's Workshop. There are many tasks that teachers must perform "behind the scenes." Frequently asked questions are:

- **What type of folders do I want students to have?** We found that the best kind of folder is a pocket folder because the students will need to store their writing in the pockets. We also found that designating the same color folder was helpful when organizing and managing materials. (i.e. The red folder is for Writer's Workshop.)

- **Where do I want the students to store folders?** We suggest that the students should not store their folders in their desks, but have a common area or container to keep them. This helps to keep the folder and writing safe.

- **How am I going to distribute the folders at the beginning of Writer's Workshop?** We found that it was most conducive to a meaningful mini-lesson to pass folders out after the mini-lesson. Then the teacher or a designated student can hand each student their writing folder before going to their silent writing place.

- **What materials do students need for Writer's Workshop?** Students will need a variety of materials in a common location. This includes paper (lined, unlined, or different colors), writing utensils, scissors, tape, and staplers. We find that a quick note to parents will often reap great rewards! Parents will send in leftover stationary, notepaper, and other writing materials if they know you need it.

- **Where am I going to store materials that students need for Writer's Workshop?** If you have a table and space, a writing table is very effective. Another option would be to store materials in containers or in another place in the room that is accessible to students. The important thing to remember is that students need to know where materials are so they don't spend valuable writing time without the tools that they need.

- **What signal should be used to help students transition?** Teachers are experts at finding the perfect tool for them. Some teachers sing a song, ring a bell, clap, play music, or use signal words. The consistency of whatever signal you choose to use makes transitions as smooth as possible.

- **When should I record the status of the class?** A teacher needs to take the status of the class every day at the same time. Some teachers choose to do this at the beginning of the class to help determine goals and conferencing objectives. However, some teachers choose to do this at the end of the writing time to monitor and assess students' progress.

• **Where should students sit to write?** This depends on the organization of the classroom, as well as the wishes of the teacher and the students. Some students write best sitting at their desk with all of their materials close at hand. Others need to be completely isolated, such as in a corner or under a table. Some need the "white noise" that is in all classrooms, and others that need total silence might want to wear earphones or mufflers. In short, students should sit and work in a location that would be most conducive to producing excellent thoughts and ideas to record.

Students have responsibilities during Writer's Workshop as well. The student must attend to the strategy work that is modeled and apply the demonstrations and think-alouds to his own writing. He must also be prepared to share his thinking as a writer during individual writing conferences or during informal chats with the teachers and his peers. Once a piece has been drafted, revised, and edited to a degree appropriate for the student skill and grade level, he shares the published writing with an audience.

Notice in the chart below the teacher has the heaviest responsibility in the mini-lesson where the whole-group instruction takes place. During the writing time, both students and teachers are actively engaged in the writing process. The sharing time spotlights the students and their writing.

	Mini-Lesson	Writing Time	Sharing Time
Teacher	• Select appropriate materials • Prepare focused lesson based on student needs • Set expectations for behavior, participation, and performance • Engage students' interest and make connections • Model procedures, skills, and strategies	• Model writing • Observe writing behaviors • Support all writers • Conference with individual students • Conference with groups of students • Supervise students during the writing process • Choose two or three students to share writing	• Model responding positively to students' writing • Celebrate successes
Students	• Attend to instruction • Participate appropriately	• Apply skills and strategies taught during mini-lesson • Follow Workshop procedures • Brainstorm • Select topic • Draft • Reread • Revise • Edit • Confer • Publish	• Share works in progress • Share published works • Contribute ideas • Ask questions about writing • Listen as other students share • Celebrate successes

The important task of successfully establishing a Writer's Workshop is dependent upon the establishing of effective routines and procedures. The phrase "a well-oiled machine" comes to mind. When classroom procedures are taught purposefully and specifically, students respond by being proud and productive authors.

Chapter 6: **What Is the Writing Process?**

Every writer knows that there is a process to writing. Often they don't realize it, but even the youngest writers begin with an idea that makes sense, and they know that the idea can be recorded. They also ensure that their writing is presented in such a way that the intended reader(s) can gain knowledge from the writing. In order to become more effective writers, it is helpful to understand the steps in the writing process.

Prewriting

So where do a writer's ideas come from? How can writers organize their thoughts in order to write well? Ideas can come from any number of sources, and some students need to be reminded of this from time to time. For most students, Mini-Lessons 1–5, listed on pages 74–80, will support students in having ideas for quite a while. If one student is out of ideas, this is best addressed in a student/teacher conference. If, however, you notice that several students are having difficulty deciding on a topic for writing, you might want to address this in a mini-lesson. An idea that has worked for us is to create a web with students. In the center of the web are the words "My ideas for writing come from . . ." Ask students to brainstorm where their ideas have come from. Some possibilities are:

- memories
- experiences
- books
- magazines
- newspapers
- the Internet
- television
- movies

- photos or pictures
- dreams
- imagination
- discussions
- interests
- research
- music

Students may also be interested in writing about people that they know. If this is the case, you could support them by brainstorming some interview questions.

When working with struggling writers, it might be helpful to visit or revisit ideas of ways to prewrite which include webbing, brainstorming, free writing, and graphic organizers. One graphic organizer that we have found to be extremely supportive is called Visualize Experience.

> "Writing taught once or twice a week is just frequent enough to remind students that they can't write and teachers that they can't teach."
>
> *–Donald Graves, 1983*

Visualize Experience

Purpose

• Use sensory experiences to activate background knowledge and to build concepts.

Example

• Ask students to close their eyes and visualize that they are attending their friend's party (or whatever setting they choose).

• Tell them to observe everything that happens because they will be writing down what they have seen. **Say:** *There are many things you might see at your friend's house. What people are there? What does the house look like? What else do you see? What sounds do you hear? Are the people laughing? What might you smell? Taste? Touch?*

• Ask students to share their observations. Write them on the chart.

At My Friend's Party	Sight	Sound	Smell	Taste	Touch
inside the house					
in the backyard					

Writing

The writing stage of your Writer's Workshop has two parts. When students are dismissed from the mini-lesson, they should go to their seats or their writing place and write silently for a predetermined amount of time. They have the choice of continuing to work on writing that they previously began or to begin a new piece of writing. With beginning writers, you might want to start with a 5-minute time period and then slowly extend the time. A timer works well for this. After the timer sounds, writers have a choice of continuing with the piece that they are writing or resuming the writing process with a previously written piece.

There is a reason for the silent writing, and this time shouldn't be skipped. It is important for students to have an opportunity to record their thoughts and ideas daily. It is possible that a student might have been involved in a response group or possibly at the publishing stage on the previous day when the Writer's Workshop concluded. If students simply resume the task that they were working on the day before, they may not have an opportunity to actually write during that workshop period or to apply what was taught during the mini-lesson.

After ideas are organized in the prewriting stage, writing time is the opportunity for students to put these ideas down on paper. Be sure to explain to help the students understand that their first attempt after the prewriting is a rough draft. Many writers struggle to understand why they are not finished when they have completed the rough draft. If many students are showing a lack of understanding, this might be a good topic for a mini-lesson. A writer is never finished! They just find something else to write about!

We like to offer students a variety of types, sizes, and colors of paper—some lined and some unlined. These items can be placed in a writing corner or on a writing table for students to get as they need them. You might want to tell students that certain paper is for the rough draft, and other paper is for the final draft or for publishing. Also located in the writing corner should be pencils, pens, and markers. You might also indicate when these tools should be used. We have tried an assortment of writing utensils, and one that seems to work well is pencils without erasers or pens with washable ink. The reason for this is, when students change their mind, they often erase until they destroy their entire paper, or they erase some excellent writing along with the error. We have occasionally seen students erase all of a completed piece of writing because they wanted to make one change.

You will want to make certain that your students understand a few basic rules about how to record their ideas on paper. These are some tried-and-true guidelines that we have used.

Students must:

- Place your name and the date on each page.
- Number the pages.
- Skip lines for revision and editing purposes.
- Write only on one side of the paper.
- Draw a line though an error or anything that you would like to change.

Teacher's Note

This would make an excellent anchor chart so students have a resource to reference.

As students begin their writing, it is essential that they maintain their initial excitement about their topic. If you notice that a student is stuck or frustrated, simply sit beside him or her for a few moments and ask how you can help. Listen carefully to the student and provide support while building the student's confidence as a writer. In almost all cases, it is not helpful to scribe for the students. If we do this, we are sending them a message: We know that they can't complete the task, so we have to do it for them.

As we circulate, conference, and support the writers in our classroom, these are a few suggestions that we want to pass along.

1. Once you start, continue to put your ideas down on paper. Revising, editing, and conferring are done after all of your thoughts are on the paper.

2. If you finish the page, get another piece of paper and continue writing until all of your ideas are on the paper.

3. You don't have to include everything that was in your prewriting. Choose only the best ideas.

4. Make sure that all sentences in the writing are about the topic.

5. Reread to make sure that your writing makes sense.

Revising

As writers complete their rough drafts, it is essential that they reread their piece of writing to make sure that it conveys the message that they intended.

Teacher's Note

This would make an excellent anchor chart so students have a resource to reference.

Students should ask themselves these questions:

- Can I read my writing aloud to a response group?
- Does my writing make sense?
- Do I need to add any information?
- Is there something in my writing that I need to take out?
- Is my writing interesting?
- Are all of my sentences complete?

Now it is time to revise the writing with a response group. The author needs to select two students that will be able to listen well and help revise the writing. The author should bring to the group his or her writing, a pencil or a pen, and a clipboard, if one is available. The other students in the group bring nothing with them. Then the three students sit knee-to-knee in a triangle in an area of the room that is designated for response groups. (There should not be more than two response groups in progress at one time.)

The students sit with the author and listen carefully. A method that has worked really well for us is the A.R.R.R. (Adding, Rearranging, Removing, Replacing) approach.

A.R.R.R.

Adding	What else does the reader need to know?
Removing	What extra details or unnecessary bits of information are in this piece of writing?
Rearranging	Is the information in the most logical and most effective order?
Replacing	What words or details could be replaced by clearer or stronger expressions?

One student can focus on anything that needs to be added or removed. The other can focus on the last two Rs—what needs to be rearranged or replaced. As the author reads his or her writing the first time, the "revisers" listen and process. Then as the author reads the piece again, the "revisers" ask the author to stop and reread or question. Afterward, the three students sit together with the draft to consider revisions, using suggestions from the "revisers" and reactions from the author. The Using Spider Legs mini-lesson (page 99) is a helpful tool in making revisions. Sometimes it is helpful for the "revisers" to ask the author for a prewriting plan in order to clarify the writing. It is important to emphasize that the "revisers" are simply providing ideas and suggestions. It is the author's prerogative to make the changes or not.

Editing

The editing stage needs to be done after revising as students' first focus must be on the content of his or her writing. Editing is the close-up view of individual sentences and words and their accuracy and clarity. When editing, the author sits with one other student who will look at the writing as the author reads it aloud. They will go through the piece together line by line, looking at each sentence, phrase, and word. Then the author will make the changes on his or her own paper. Most students are very possessive and very proud of their writing. Authors must understand that they are the only ones to decide what changes should be made to their writing.

Some things that editors might check for are:

- Are the sentences grammatically correct?
- Are all punctuation marks in place?
- Are words spelled correctly?
- Has the same word been used too many times?
- Are any of the sentences hard to understand?

Remember that students should only be responsible for mechanics and conventions that they have been taught, so, when editing, you can expect that they will use the punctuation that you have taught, and they will spell correctly the high-frequency words that you are certain that they know, as well as all words on the word wall.

When the peer editing is completed, the student then signs the "Confer with the Teacher" notebook. When the teacher meets with the author, the goal is to support the student in making his or her writing completely ready for publication. Teachers have a fine line to walk when talking about having a piece ready for publication. Making a piece as perfect as possible is important so students realize that a published piece is "readable" to his or her audience. It is vital, however, that the student makes any changes to his or her own paper so that there is a connection to the teaching. The teacher should not overwhelm the student with many additional edits and revisions. Remember to choose only one or two teaching points that are the most important for that student. If students will publish using a word processor, we often go back and make editing changes before printing. If a student is going to be writing his or her published piece by hand, correct spelling, modeled correct punctuation, or revised sentences are written on self-stick notes or on additional pieces of paper for the student to use as references as they are rewriting.

Publishing

The final step of the writing process is publication. This means different things to different authors, depending on the piece they are working on. Students will simply need to produce a final copy of their work in the format of their choice. This might mean adding a cover, a title page, a biographical sketch, an index, pictures, photos, and captions. It might mean transferring the draft to a chart or a poster. Bloggers would upload and post their piece of completed work to a class website. This stage of the process becomes a time of joy for writers as they begin to see the fruits of their labors. Move students to this stage early in the school year in order to clarify their concept of and feelings about the entire process. Once they understand the excitement of publishing, the process can slow down and become more thorough on subsequent pieces.

Sharing

When sharing a published piece, students are very proud of their efforts, whether it is their first publication or their twentieth. They need a forum to share and to receive recognition and acclaim. The author's chair should be reserved for students who have published their writing. At the beginning of the year, when the first author sits in the chair and shares his or her writing, it is amazing what an incentive this is for the other students!

During sharing time, the author's responsibility is to show his or her writing and to read it in a voice that can be clearly understood by the other students. In addition, the author should be prepared to answer questions after the reading.

The audience has responsibilities, as well, and these may be the subject of a few mini-lessons.

The audience should:

- Listen carefully

- Form questions that pertain to the writing

- Consider positive, constructive comments to make to the author

We have used mini-lessons to brainstorm sentence starters and record them on an anchor chart so that students will understand what it means to make a positive comment and how that differs from a question. Some suggestions for an anchor chart are:

Questions:

- How did you _____?

- Why did you _____?

- Why did your character _____?

- What do you think happened next?

- Why did you begin your story with _____?

- Why did your story end with _____?

- Can you tell me more about _____?

Comments:

- I really like when _____.

- I enjoyed this writing because _____.

- I liked the part about _____ because _____.

- The ending was interesting because _____.

- The beginning of your story really caught my attention because _____.

We usually let students take their published work home to share with their families. They were then required to return it to school the next day. Students' books and other publications were then placed in a reading corner in the room so that other students could enjoy these materials during independent reading time. Students can even record their books, and a tape could be placed with the book at a listening station.

Five Stages of the Writing Process

Primary Grades

Prewriting
- Choosing a topic
- Organizing thoughts
- Telling ideas orally
- Brainstorming, listing, webbing, and charting

Drafting
- Referring to prewriting
- Developing the topic
- Communicating meaning
- Recording the flow of ideas in logical order

Revising
- Rereading the draft and choosing ways to make it better
- Sharing and conferring for feedback
- Adding, removing, rearranging, and replacing ideas, words, phrases, and sentences
- Checking sentence structure
- Checking word usage
- Utilizing feedback from peers

Editing
- Checking spelling
- Checking capitalization
- Checking punctuation

Publishing
- Presenting in final form to an audience

The drawing below demonstrates the non-linear nature of the writing process. Real writing is recursive and loops back to other parts of the process throughout its efforts to communicate meaning.

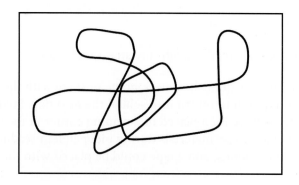

Five Stages of the Writing Process

Intermediate Grades

Prewriting
- Choosing a topic
- Organizing thoughts
- Creating clusters, semantic maps, flowcharts, or other forms of graphic planners
- Taking notes
- Considering the purpose of the piece
- Considering the audience of the piece

Drafting
- Referring to prewriting or graphic planner
- Developing the topic
- Determining point of view
- Emphasizing content
- Organizing, reorganizing, and reflecting as writing unfolds

Revising
- Rereading the draft and choosing ways to make it better
- Sharing and conferring for feedback
- Adding, removing, rearranging, and replacing ideas, words, phrases, and sentences
- Elaborating upon ideas
- Reconsidering and clarifying the structure or sequence of events
- Adding, removing, rearranging, and replacing ideas, words, phrases, and sentences
- Elaborating upon ideas
- Considering sentence structure and word choice
- Keeping at it until satisfied

Editing
- Looking for mechanical errors, such as spelling, grammar, and punctuation
- Conferring with teacher and partner about mechanics

Publishing
- Considering both formal and informal venues
- Delivering the text to a wider audience
- Polishing the piece to go public
- Typing, creating bound books, illustrating

The drawing here demonstrates the non-linear nature of the writing process. Real writing is recursive and loops back to other parts of the process throughout its efforts to communicate meaning.

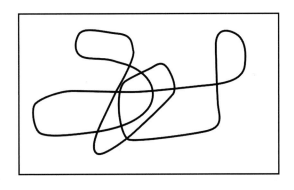

Revision Checklist

Name_____ Date_____

Title of Piece_____

❏ I have reread my piece, and it makes sense.

❏ I have read my draft to two friends and listened to their suggestions.

❏ I have improved my draft.

- -

Revision Checklist

Name_____ Date_____

Title of Piece_____

❏ I have reread my piece, and it makes sense.

❏ I have read my draft to two friends and listened to their suggestions.

❏ I have improved my draft.

- -

Revision Checklist

Name_____ Date_____

Title of Piece_____

❏ I have reread my piece, and it makes sense.

❏ I have read my draft to two friends and listened to their suggestions.

❏ I have improved my draft.

Editing Checklist

Name_____ Date_____

Title of Piece_____

❑ I have reread my piece to make sure words are spelled correctly.

❑ I have reread my piece to make sure I have used punctuation correctly.

❑ I have read my piece with a classmate. We checked over my piece to make sure I used correct spelling and punctuation.

- -

Editing Checklist

Name_____ Date_____

Title of Piece_____

❑ I have reread my piece to make sure words are spelled correctly.

❑ I have reread my piece to make sure I have used punctuation correctly.

❑ I have read my piece with a classmate. We checked over my piece to make sure I used correct spelling and punctuation.

- -

Editing Checklist

Name_____ Date_____

Title of Piece_____

❑ I have reread my piece to make sure words are spelled correctly.

❑ I have reread my piece to make sure I have used punctuation correctly.

❑ I have read my piece with a classmate. We checked over my piece to make sure I used correct spelling and punctuation.

Chapter 7: **How Does Conferencing With a Student Look?**

A Writer's Workshop without conferences is like a football team trying to play a game without the coach. The teacher's role in a Workshop is critical. She establishes the environment, plans the instruction, monitors the needs of students, and coaches them one by one. Having gained a good understanding of the students and their motivations, challenges, and strengths, the classroom teacher has great potential for moving young writers forward. Much of this progress will come through individual contact in conferences.

The purpose of a writing conference is to provide individual attention to student writers at their points of need. At any given moment, different students will be prewriting, drafting, revising, editing, and polishing pieces for publication, so they will have different needs. During writing time, students have the opportunity to meet with their teacher for support on their particular pieces.

The teacher's role is to read or listen to the writer's piece, help him determine the intended audience, and respond in ways that prompt him to see the piece from that perspective. The teacher does not prescribe a "fix" for "broken" writing, but instead asks the right questions so that the writer can draw his or her own conclusions on how to best improve the piece. The student's role is to be engaged in writing, be willing to listen to feedback and questioning about the piece, and be willing to revise, if necessary, based on new learning.

The teacher's ability to spend 3–5 minutes in an uninterrupted conversation with a student writer depends heavily on the establishment of certain classroom norms. Two important aspects of the classroom environment must be in place before conferencing can be effective. First, the Workshop must be running smoothly, with a manageable noise level, and students must be capable of working independently in their writing. If students are behaving disrespectfully, talking loudly, or relying too heavily on the teacher for decision-making, the teacher's attempts at conferring with individual students will fail. Each of these issues can be addressed in a procedural mini-lesson and individual conferences with misbehaving students. Procedural mini-lessons occur daily during the early days of Workshop and are repeated as often as necessary throughout the year to ensure a quality block of instructional time. Second, the students must gain an understanding of the audience for their pieces. Without concern for the opinions of their readers, students' motivation for revising and improving their work will be slight. Building a sense of audience in all students happens best through two particular means.

- Reading literature and discussing the attributes of the writing causes the students to be more aware of the reader's role in writing.

- Once students experience the process of publishing a piece and sharing it with an audience, the feedback they receive quickly shapes their motivation for continued writing.

> Once students experience the process of publishing a piece and sharing it with an audience, the feedback they receive quickly shapes their motivation for continued writing.

While an observer in a Workshop classroom might mistake a writing conference for a friendly, informal conversation, the exchange is actually a sophisticated teaching interaction designed to move students forward in their writing. Through listening to the student's stated needs and attending to his or her developing piece of writing, the teacher provides a sincere response to the student's message and questions him or her in ways that cause the student to look at his or her writing from the reader's perspective. During a writing conference, Donald Graves (1994) states that students should do 80 percent of the talking and a teacher should do 20 percent. As students talk through their intentions and dilemmas, their ideas crystallize and they are better able to determine the writing's course.

It is important for a teacher to remember three key sections of a writing conference. At the beginning of the conference, the teacher's purpose is to get the student talking. This is also called the "research" phase of a conference. During the early moments of the exchange, ask the student carefully worded, open-ended questions about the work. The question "How is your writing going today?" will get an entirely different response than the question "What is the title of your piece?" The first inquiry demonstrates interest in both the progress of the piece and the process of writing it, including the student's intentions and planning strategies. As the student answers, it is likely that his or her immediate writing concerns will surface as well as a few less obvious issues. Sometimes students are capable of vocalizing their progress and concerns, and sometimes they are not. If they don't have a response, encourage them to read the piece aloud and discuss how they reached their current point in the story. Use that information to formulate the approach in the second phase of the conference.

The second phase of the conference, or the middle of the conference, is a time to listen, comment, and prompt the student. After listening to the student during the first phase of the conference, you now have a better idea of the issues at hand. Some of the things you may question are:

- Is the student stalled?
- Are there problems with selecting a topic of interest?
- Is the student having trouble seeing areas that need revision?
- Is the draft coherent?
- Is the piece focused on one big idea or littered with several competing thoughts?
- Does the student have an investment in the topic?
- Would it help to see additional samples of writing in their particular genre?

Teachers who clearly understand the writing process and have grappled with writing themselves will be best able to know the most appropriate next step. Decide on one or two areas that need attention, and then decide how to support them. Consider what you are looking for in the final writing product, based on recent mini-lessons. Is it structure, organization and focus, a growing control of conventions, voice, or the ability to emulate a favorite author? Question the student in ways that lead toward your objectives. Don't be tempted to point out every issue their writing. Instead, ask yourself, "Of all that I could teach this student, what would make the biggest difference right now?"

Consider Lev Vygotsky's "zone of proximal development" theory which asserts that students working with skills that are not too difficult or too easy will make progress with the help of a skilled coach who can scaffold their learning. Some have summarized this theory by saying, "What a student can do with help today, he can do alone tomorrow." This theory has a direct application to working with students during conferences. The middle section of a conference—where the teachable moment takes place—is the opportunity to help move the writer one step closer to the goals of good writing. During the middle of the conference, use these tips to help you in the commenting and prompting process:

- Respond by saying, "Your reader might think . . ." rather than "I think . . ." This phrase focuses the student's attention on:
  —how others respond to the writing,
  —how others perceive the writing, and
  —the importance of the audience to the final product.

- Do not use a pen to mark corrections. When needed, self-stick notes can be affixed to the student's work without diminishing either the writer or the writing.

At the end of the conference, draw it to a close by prompting the student toward a specific next action. For example, say, "I think you see now how the sequence might be confusing, so please rearrange the sections we discussed." The reminder needn't be drawn out or preachy but should nudge the student back into work and eliminate any sidetracking that might occur as the teacher moves on to the next student.

A good rule of thumb for conferences is "short and often." When conferences remain brief—three to five minutes—the teacher has a chance to meet with at least five to ten writers during the Writer's Workshop. This helps maintain close contact on a regular basis with all writers as they work through their individual processes.

Countless exchanges occur between teachers and students in Writer's Workshop. It is difficult to characterize one conversation as an official "conference" while another is just a discussion. Frequent communication between all participants is key. In the instructional context, however, it helps to realize all of the available options for conferences.

Types of Conferences

There are five types of Writer's Workshop conferences. These conferences are each unique in their own way, but the main objective is to use the type of conference that will help an author grow in their writing. The first type of conference is a **teacher-initiated conference**. This is where a teacher selects approximately five students to meet with daily. The conference last about three to five minutes with each student. The objective of the teacher is to meet with all of the students in class once or twice a week. The student's role is to read the current writing piece aloud and bring up a question or area that needs attention. The teacher's role is to provide specific, positive feedback about the strengths of the piece and provide limited feedback to the question raised by the writer as well as no more than one other aspect of the writing that needs attention. The teacher also keeps brief anecdotal records about the conference for future reference.

Another type of conference is the **student-initiated conference**. In order to implement student-initiated conferences in the classroom, the teacher uses a procedural mini-lesson to explain the process by which students may initiate conferences with the teacher. Students with pressing questions or concerns sign up on a "request a conference" sheet (see page 46). While waiting for the conference, students continue writing on their current piece of writing. The teacher then reserves five to ten minutes at the end of the writing time to confer with these students. If this isn't enough time, then the teacher arranges other times during the day to continue one or two of the conferences so the timeliness of the question doesn't pass.

The third type of conference is the **teacher-scheduled small-group conference**. When a teacher determines a common need among a group of two to six students, it is appropriate to schedule a small-group conference. The small group gathers around a table or on the floor so the teacher can review the common challenge with the students. During this time, the teacher asks guiding questions to help students see solutions and prompts them to return to work and apply the information. This conference lasts three to five minutes and addresses one issue or problem at a time.

The fourth type of conference is the **status conference**. The status conference is a time when the teacher uses the daily information gained from taking the status of the class to confer with students who are not making progress with their writing.

The last type of conference is a **peer conference**. A peer conference is when a student visits with another student about their writing. The students are taught the types of questions to visit about during mini-lessons. Some of these questions could include:

- What is the piece about?
- Is any part of the piece confusing?
- What do I like best about the piece?
- What do I want to know more about?

The teacher also establishes a procedure for initiating a peer conference. This would include the writer using criteria for deciding the need for a conference. Reasons a writer might ask for a peer conference are:

- What should come next? (Am I stalled at a point in my writing?)
- The draft is finished and needs to be heard.
- Revisions have been made and the piece needs to be reread.

The teacher would designate an area of the room to be used for the conferences since this may produce an added noise level. The teacher also models the way a conference looks. The peer responders listen to a piece twice—once to grasp the meaning, and once to determine appropriate feedback. It is important that the teacher is aware so that it is possible to redirect any off-task and inappropriate behavior. The students' goal is to focus on the overall objective of becoming better writers.

Questioning Strategies

It has been said that teaching is an art and a science. If this is true, then questioning falls into both categories. In order to utilize questioning strategies, teachers must have a clear understanding of quality writing and the process used to achieve it. They must also understand the nuances in their student's personalities, developmental abilities, and sensitivities. It is important that teachers be able to phrase a question in a way that promotes thinking rather than one particular answer and that the questions are appropriate to different skill levels. When a teacher is asking questions during a writing conference, consideration of the piece of writing as well as the personality of the student will help determine the types of questions asked.

Some examples of questions are:

- What are you working on?
- How's it going?
- Where are you in your writing?
- What can I do to help you?
- What is your best part? Why do you like it?
- Where are you having trouble?
- How can you solve that problem?
- Can you read that aloud again and see how it sounds?
- The reader might be a little confused here. Can you explain it?
- How else might you say that?
- I loved the part about _____. Can you tell me more about it?
- You added so many more details when you told me the story. How could you add some of those to your piece to paint a better picture for your reader?

It is so important to remember that as you respond to your students' writing, be sure to respond from the perspective of "the reader" rather than a "teacher." Your goal as a teacher is to help the student understand the importance of writing for a real audience and help students respond to the needs of a reader.

Organization and Record Keeping Tools

In any given workshop session, it is common for a teacher to confer with ten or more students in formal or informal interactions. It would be impossible to keep track of what you said to whom without keeping and organizing records. Following are descriptions of some forms you can utilize in order to make effective use of conference information.

Status of the Class (see page 44) (Atwell, 1998)—helps you get an overall feel for where the students are working.

Student-Scheduled Conference Form (see page 45) (Dorn and Soffus, 2001)—documents the titles of the students' pieces, the point at which they confer with the teacher, and whether the piece is ultimately published.

Student Conference Planning Form (see page 46)—helps students clarify their thinking before a conference by recording the working title, the issues they may need help with, and the stage of the process they've reached.

Teacher-Scheduled Conference Form (see page 48) (Dorn and Soffus, 2001)—documents students that the teacher confers with, the stage they've reached in their writing, and brief notes about topics discussed in their writing.

Daily or weekly, a teacher's role is to review conference notes to plan for instruction in the Workshop, allowing conference topics to guide mini-lesson topics. Conference notes also help as you confer with parents and document progress as you point out the dates and content you worked on individually with a student. It also demonstrates the quality of instruction students receive in Writer's Workshop.

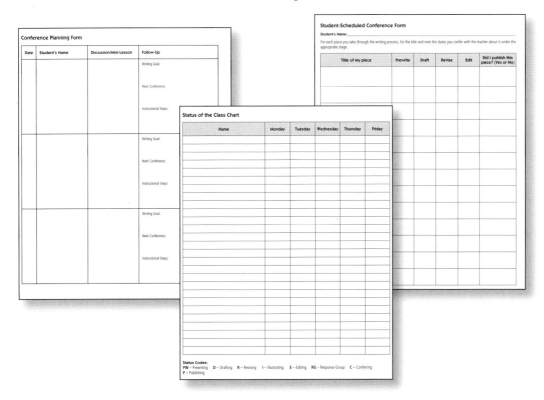

Status of the Class Chart

Name	Monday	Tuesday	Wednesday	Thursday	Friday

Status Codes:
PW – Prewriting   **D** – Drafting   **R** – Revising   **I** – Illustrating   **E** – Editing   **RG** – Response Group   **C** – Conferring
P – Publishing

Student-Scheduled Conference Form

Student's Name:_____

For each piece you take through the writing process, list the title and note the dates you confer with the teacher about it under the appropriate stage.

Title of my piece	Prewrite	Draft	Revise	Edit	Did I publish this piece? (Yes or No)

Student Planning Conference Form

Student name: _____

Title: _____

Stage of process: _____

I need help with: _____

- -

Student Planning Conference Form

Student name: _____

Title: _____

Stage of process: _____

I need help with: _____

- -

Student Planning Conference Form

Student name: _____

Title: _____

Stage of process: _____

I need help with: _____

- -

Student Planning Conference Form

Student name: _____

Title: _____

Stage of process: _____

I need help with: _____

Student Anecdotal Record Sheet

Name: Date:	Name: Date:	Name: Date:	Name: Date:	Name: Date:
Name: Date:	Name: Date:	Name: Date:	Name: Date:	Name: Date:
Name: Date:	Name: Date:	Name: Date:	Name: Date:	Name: Date:
Name: Date:	Name: Date:	Name: Date:	Name: Date:	Name: Date:

Conference Planning Form

Date	Student's Name	Discussion/Mini-Lesson	Follow-Up
			Writing Goal: Next Conference: Instructional Steps:
			Writing Goal: Next Conference: Instructional Steps:
			Writing Goal: Next Conference: Instructional Steps:

Writing Conference Questions

Starting the Conference:
- Where are you in the writing process?
- How are you using today's mini-lesson strategy in your personal writing?
- How is it going?
- What parts are going well for you?
- What parts are giving you problems?
- What is your topic? Are there subtopics that you want to address?
- What is the main idea you want to get across?
- How is this genre supporting your idea?
- Who will be your audience?

Going Deeper:
- What additional data do you need?
- Have you received responses to your piece from classmates?
- What can you add or delete to make your message clearer?
- How will you know when you are ready to edit?
- How do you want your published piece to look?

Ending the Conference:
- What is your writing goal?
- How do you plan to apply this goal to your writing?
- Which mini-lesson strategies are you consistently using?
- How have these strategies helped you to improve as a writer?
- What questions do you have?
- What would you like to discuss at our next conference?

Chapter 8: **What Is Meant by Publishing?**

Celebrate! That's what comes to mind when we think about students as they publish the writing that they have created, developed, and refined. We've looked into students' eyes, watched students listen to others' writing, and we have seen a student's pride when they share a piece of published writing. Publishing, to us, is like the icing on the cake. It's the final and most visible product of all of the hard work authors put into a book, an article, or any piece of writing. Just remember—there's no one right way to publish a student's writing.

This makes us think of the time we walked into a Grade 3 teacher's classroom. We were there to help her get her Writer's Workshop started. We started reading the responses her class had written to *Charlotte's Web* that were displayed on the wall. It was obvious that the students had been instructed on the elements of a thoughtful response because the content was excellent. The writing, however, left much to be desired. We observed sloppy handwriting, misspelled words, errors in punctuation, and many other editing errors. When we talked with the teacher, we expressed how excited we were to see so many great thoughts and ideas coming from the students. We explained that the errors had an effect on us as readers of their writing. We were distracted from the content because we had to spend so much time and energy deciphering the meaning of the responses because of poor spelling, penmanship, and punctuation.

Does a student's writing need to be perfect when "published" for all to see?

When we invite students to look at a published book, do they notice mechanical errors? Was this writing edited with the reader in mind? The answers to these questions are obvious. A published piece of writing should be as perfect as we can make it. We want readers to be able to enjoy published work, and they will struggle if mechanical errors make comprehension difficult.

Will every piece of writing be published?

An issue every writing teacher needs to address is that of abandoning pieces of writing. Sometimes students lose interest in writing a piece, get stuck or confused in the middle of the writing, or have something else they want to write about. If so, they may temporarily or permanently abandon a piece of writing. It is important for a student to realize that it is acceptable to abandon a piece—as long as this doesn't become a habit. While reviewing the status of the class or during student/teacher conferences, it may be evident that a student is continuously abandoning pieces of writing. If so, it will become necessary to have a conference to explain the importance of taking a piece of writing to publication. If many students are abandoning their writing, it could become necessary to address this in a mini-lesson for the whole class.

It is important for a student to publish! Not only does it give the student a well-deserved sense of accomplishment, but it also gives the teacher a "portfolio" to document students' growth. This feeling of celebration that students feel is invaluable as they think of themselves as authors. It is also a wonderful motivation for students who are still in earlier stages of the writing process and who are working toward the goal of a published piece.

Should there be a required number of times a student must publish?

It's difficult to determine if there should be a certain number of published pieces during a specific time. Most of the time, unless an amount is predetermined by the school district or another authority, there should be no "stick of measurement" on the number of published pieces. This is where differentiation must be considered. We don't want to encourage the student who is involved in writing a fabulous fifty-page novel to feel pressured to turn out several mediocre six-page short stories. The value is the growth of the writer. This is definitely a case of quality vs. quantity. The number of published pieces will be different for different students.

What different types of writing should be encouraged during Writer's Workshop?

Your school or district may require different genres to be studied at different grade levels. Your mini-lessons will reflect these genres. The teacher will want to model and encourage different genres during the mini-lessons, but students have the power of choice. Mini-lessons may motivate students to experiment with their writing in some of the following genres:

- Personal narrative
- Biography
- Historical fiction
- Realistic fiction
- Poetry
- Science fiction
- Mythology
- Book review

- Book/Movie/ Television review
- Fairy tale
- Fable
- Research project
- Letter
- Memoir
- Mystery

What are some of the ways students can publish their writing?

There are few limits on the ways a published piece can appear. Different genres will lend themselves to different ways of publication. Many students will want to publish in book format.

Here are some book publishing ideas:

- Books that are bound with a plastic binding with construction paper covers
- Books that are hole-punched and tied with yarn
- Books with hard covers made from cereal boxes or tag board and covered with shelf paper
- Books stapled together
- Shape books
- Notebook
- Pattern books

There are many other ways students can publish their writing. These may include:

- Posters
- Threefold brochures
- Charts
- Newspaper articles
- Plays
- Blogs

Some teachers may ask students to contribute to a class anthology where each student's writing is featured. We have seen class anthologies of poetry, biographies, short stories, and theme-based writing. Students treasure these books throughout the year. Some schools then choose to place these books in the central library where students of all grades can enjoy the writing.

Some teachers let students use computers to type their own pieces of writing for publication, and other teachers ask volunteers to help type these pieces. Some feel that typing the piece gives the student one more chance to peruse their writing and have an opportunity to practice keyboarding, and others feel that a student's time should be spent beginning a new piece of writing while their finished piece is being typed by an adult. Many teachers give their students a choice of having a typed piece for publication or writing their piece using their very best handwriting. Some of the pieces are short, while others are quite lengthy. Most published pieces have spaces left for students to add illustrations that enhance the visual quality of their published piece. The wonderful part of publishing is that there are so many good choices! Students love being in control of how their finished product will look.

What do I do with my students' published pieces?

We usually celebrated after a piece was published during sharing time. This involved having the author sit in a special place designated as the author's chair. The class gathered around to hear the author read his or her writing. This was definitely the author's "time to shine!" The class asked questions of the author, gave glowing reviews, and watched as the author "autographed" the published work. The published writing was then sent home to be shared with family, and the expectation was that it would soon be returned to take its place of honor in the classroom with other published works. We also held a yearly celebration called the "Author's Tea." We invited parents and family to hear each student read a piece of his or her own writing. A fun time was had by all!

Some teachers have a celebration twice a year or once per grading period. Other opportunities to celebrate authors may include:

- Mother's Day

- Father's Day

- Seasonal changes
  (Fall Festival of Authors, Winter Wonderland of Writing, Spring Into Writing)

- Birthdays

Perhaps the message about publishing is not the method of publishing or what the finished product looks like, but that the writing is celebrated and valued! The purpose is that students see themselves as authors.

Chapter 9: How Do We Assess Students' Writing During Writer's Workshop?

One of our very dear friends told us a story about an experience he had in Kindergarten. He was told to draw a picture, and then write a sentence about the moon. He recalled a funny story about the moon being made of green cheese. He decided to tell the funny story to his teacher by drawing a picture of a green moon and then writing about it. He gave his paper to the teacher expecting a laugh or smile, but instead she handed it back with a scowl and said, "What's the matter with you? The moon is not green! Your homework tonight is to go outside and look at the moon. Then you need to draw your picture and write your sentence correctly." He's a very successful professional who has no confidence in himself as a writer because he was judged as less than adequate as a child. This causes us to reflect on the impact our comments have on students. How amazing that our friend remembers this experience to this day. As teachers, our quick words and judgments can affect our students for life.

The question becomes, how do we assess our students in a constructive way? There are two things to think about.

- What purpose does the assessment serve?
- What tools should teachers use to perform assessments?

The main purpose of assessment in Writer's Workshop is to help teachers make informed decisions about instruction. From the information teachers gain from various assessments, they should be able to support and guide students as they grow as writers, document growth, select an instructional focus, determine students' strengths and weaknesses, and provide a writing grade.

Students are unique, so moving students towards appropriate goals is one of a teacher's most important roles during Writer's Workshop. Teachers may find that anecdotal notes are an effective way of documenting a student's progress. We have found that self-stick notes and a clipboard work well for this purpose. While observing students during writing time and during conferences, we like to document the student's name, date, and any instruction that was needed. We also noted what the student was doing well and any teaching points that we made during the conversation with the student.

3-2 David	**11-22 Jennifer**
• Needs help with story lead • Good use of adjectives • Conference focus— elaboration	• Conference focus—complete sentence • Picture matched writing • Needs help with spacing

Teachers may want to create portfolios containing samples of students' writing to document growth. Portfolios may be useful when discussing students' progress with administrators, coaches, and parents. Students' strengths and weakness can also be noted in a portfolio. It is important to keep in mind that a grade should never be placed on a student's published work; however, teachers can use rubrics or checklists with students' work in the portfolios to determine criteria for a grade.

We are including some rubrics and checklists that may be used as anecdotal notes or as appropriate formative assessments. Please see pages 57–60 for primary grades and pages 61–62 for intermediate grades.

Use of This Rubric: If it is necessary for teachers to assess students' writing for a grade, the teacher can use this rubric as he or she reflects on several different examples of students' writing, anecdotal notes, informal observations, as well as the students' developmental levels.

The criteria that are listed in the left-hand column are elements that have been well-addressed during mini-lessons, and therefore, it is expected that most students will able to transfer these skills and strategies to their writing.

Sample Portfolio Rubric

	1 No evidence of the skill	2 Attempt to apply skill is evident, but more work is needed	3 Very good; slight room for improvement	4 Excellent
Included a lead that captured the reader's attention				Three different pieces had excellent leads.
Included a logical sequence of ideas or events			Stories are showing improvement logical order. Needs improvement in use of sequence words for clarity.	
All sentences had appropriate end punctuation		Little consistent use of end punctuation, making the pieces difficult to understand.		
Contained at least one example of dialogue between characters in the story				Excellent use of conversation, which deepened the reader's understanding of the personal narrative and the mystery story.
			Total points:	13

Individual Writing Observation Record – Emergent

Name: _____ Date: _____

	Beginning	Progressing	Proficient
Forms letters correctly			
Uses spaces between words			
Articulates words slowly and identifies sound/symbol relationships			
Writes high-frequency words fluently			
Analyzes and records a few sounds in words			
Rereads message to confirm and extend message			
Edits by crossing out words that do not look right			
Analyzes sounds in sequence and records what is heard			
Self-corrects misspelled words using various resources			
Applies knowledge of visual patterns to write new words			
Uses meaningful chunks (-s, -ed, -ing)			
Increases writing vocabulary			

Group Writing Observation Record – Emergent

Name: _____ Date: _____

Emergent/Early Writing Behaviors	Student Names								Comments/Concerns
Forms letters correctly									
Uses spaces between words									
Articulates words slowly									
Writes high-frequency words fluently									
Analyzes and records a few sounds in words									
Uses alphabet chart to make connections with sounds and letters									
Reads to confirm and extend message									
Edits by crossing out words that do not look right									
Analyzes sounds in sequence									
Self-corrects misspelled words									
Applies knowledge of visual patterns to write new words									
Uses meaningful chunks (-s, -ed, -ing)									

Individual Writing Observation Record – Early Level

Name: _____ Date: _____

Writing Sample Rubric Scores:

Content/Ideas _____   Organization _____   Voice/Style _____   Mechanics _____

Chart Coding Legend:

✓   writing behaviors at the proficient stage of development

X   writing behaviors at the progressing stage of development

−   writing behaviors at the beginning stage of development

	Beginning	Progressing	Proficient
Uses analogy to write unknown words			
Records unknown words using syllables			
Writing vocabulary includes new and unusual words			
Longer messages are composed with greater accuracy			
Initiates problem-solving on unknown words in various ways			
Revises content and word choices in message			
Uses a variety of punctuation			
Edits writing for spelling and punctuation			

Group Writing Observation Record – Early Level

Name: _____ **Date:** _____

Chart Coding Legend:

√ writing behaviors at the proficient stage of development

X writing behaviors at the progressing stage of development

– writing behaviors at the beginning stage of development

	Student Names								Comments/Concerns
Emergent/Early Writing Behaviors									
Uses analogies to write unknown words									
Records unknown words using syllables									
Writing vocabulary includes new and unusual words									
Longer messages are composed with greater accuracy									
Initiates problem-solving on unknown words in various ways									
Revises content and word choices in message									
Uses a variety of punctuation									
Edits writing for spelling and punctuation									

Individual Writing Observation Record – Fluent Level

Name: _____ Date: _____

Writing Sample Rubric Scores: Content Ideas _____ Organization _____ Voice/Style _____ Mechanics _____

Competency	Beginning	Progressing	Proficient
Writing Process			
Generates ideas for composing			
Uses brainstorming and ordering and/or graphic organizers to plan a topic			
Produces more than one draft			
Revises writing for content and clarity			
Edits writing for capitalization			
Edits writing for punctuation			
Edits writing for standard grammar			
Edits writing for spelling			
Writing Craft			
Uses appropriate format in writing (e.g., margins, titles, etc.)			
Incorporates the craft of writing, such as style and language, into writing			
Uses various ways to communicate, such as learning logs, semantic maps, lists, books			
Demonstrates success in writing personal narratives			
Demonstrates success in writing expository text			
Demonstrates success in writing poetry			
Demonstrates success in writing stories			
Maintains a writing folder			
Writes spontaneously			
Uses a variety of resources, such as a dictionary and a thesaurus			

Group Writing Observation Record – Fluent Level

Name: _____ **Date:** _____

Chart Coding Legend:

√ writing behaviors at the proficient stage of development

X writing behaviors at the progressing stage of development

– writing behaviors at the beginning stage of development

Writing Behaviors	Student Names								Comments/Concerns
Writing Process									
Generates ideas for composing									
Uses brainstorming and ordering and/or graphic organizers to plan a topic									
Produces more than one draft									
Revises writing for content and clarity									
Edits writing for capitalization									
Edits writing for punctuation									
Edits writing for standard grammar									
Edits writing for spelling									
Writing Craft									
Uses appropriate format in writing (e.g., margins, titles, etc.)									
Incorporates the craft of writing, such as style and language, into writing									
Uses various ways to communicate, such as learning logs, semantic maps, lists, books									
Demonstrates success in writing personal narratives									
Demonstrates success in writing expository text									
Demonstrates success in writing poetry									
Demonstrates success in writing stories									
Maintains a writing folder									
Writes spontaneously									
Uses a variety of resources, such as a dictionary and a thesaurus									

Individual Expository Writing Assessment Record

Name: _____ **Date:** _____

Text Title: _____ **Level:** _____

Rubric

1. Includes minimal information in writing
2. Includes moderate information in writing
3. Includes complete information in writing

	Rubric	Comments/Concerns
Uses graphic organizer to plan and organize		
Explains the topic		
Provides details to support the topic		
Compares the topic, using details, in similarity and difference		
States the cause and effect		
Provides detail in appropriate sequence		
Uses paragraphs to group like information together		
Uses clear descriptions		
Explains how the topic has personal relevance		

Group Expository Writing Assessment Record

Name: _____   Date: _____

Text Title: _____   Level: _____   Theme: _____

Rubric 1. Includes minimal information in writing 2. Includes moderate information in writing 3. Includes complete information in writing	Student Names									
Uses graphic organizer to plan and organize										
Explains the topic										
Provides details to support the topic										
Compares the topic, using details, in similarity and difference										
States the cause and effect										
Provides detail in appropriate sequence										
Uses clear descriptions										
Explains how the topic has personal relevance										
Uses meaningful chunks (-s, -ed, -ing)										

Individual Writing Observation Record

Name: _____ Date: _____

Rubric Score: _____

Competency	Beginning	Progressing	Proficient
Writing Process			
Generates ideas for composing			
Uses brainstorming and ordering and/or graphic organizers to plan a topic			
Produces more than one draft			
Revises writing for content and clarity			
Edits writing for capitalization			
Edits writing for punctuation			
Edits writing for standard grammar			
Edits writing for spelling			
Writing Craft			
Uses appropriate format in writing (e.g., margins, titles, etc.)			
Incorporates the craft of writing, such as style and language, into writing			
Uses various ways to communicate, such as learning logs, semantic maps, lists, books			
Demonstrates success in writing personal narratives			
Demonstrates success in writing expository text			
Demonstrates success in writing poetry			
Demonstrates success in writing stories			
Maintains a writing folder			
Writes spontaneously			
Uses a variety of resources, such as a dictionary and a thesaurus			
Writing Behaviors			
Constructs words using larger chunks of graphophonic information			
Uses familiar graphophonic patterns when writing			
Manipulates onsets and rhymes when writing unfamiliar words			
Uses new and familiar words when writing			
Composes longer texts			
Writes for various audiences and purposes			

©2012 Benchmark Education Company, LLC

Individual Writing Observation Record

Name: _____ Date: _____

Rubric Score: _____

Competency	Beginning	Progressing	Proficient
Links Prior Knowledge			
Uses prewriting strategies to activate prior knowledge (brainstorming, graphic organizers, collects data			
Relates prior experiences to the topic			
Makes connections about the topic to other books			
Makes connections about the topic to prior knowledge of the topic			
Audience/Purpose			
Identifies specific purpose for writing			
Identifies appropriate text features and organization for the writing			
Identifies appropriate audience and format			
Composition			
Writing includes beginning, middle, end			
Main ideas are clear and fully developed			
Main ideas are supported with details			
Categorizes ideas and forms paragraphs			
Paragraphs have a logical sequence			
Each paragraph includes topic sentence, supporting details, and concluding sentence			
Uses transitions to move from one idea to the next idea			
Uses descriptive language to hold readers' attention and to develop imagery			
Stays on the topic			
Expresses feelings in writing			
Develops good leads			

Individual Writer's Workshop Observation Record

Name _____   Date _____

Title of Writing Sample/Project _____   Genre _____

Writing Process Stage _____   Date of Completion _____

Writing Conference Notes

Validation _____   _____

Activation _____   _____

Comments _____   _____

Next Focus for Instruction:

- -

Name _____   Date _____

Title of Writing Sample/Project _____   Genre _____

Writing Process Stage _____   Date of Completion _____

Writing Conference Notes

Validation _____   _____

Activation _____   _____

Comments _____   _____

Next Focus for Instruction:

- -

Name _____   Date _____

Title of Writing Sample/Project _____   Genre _____

Writing Process Stage _____   Date of Completion _____

Writing Conference Notes

Validation _____   _____

Activation _____   _____

Comments _____   _____

Next Focus for Instruction:

Group Writer's Workshop Observation Record

Date(s) of Observations _____

Name	Title	Genre	Writing Process Stage	Conference Notes	Date Completed

Chapter 10: How Do Teachers Select and Create Mini-Lessons?

. . . and 45 minutes later, the mini-lesson ends. Some of the students are glassy-eyed and others are off-task. The teacher is exhausted, and confusion reigns because so many different topics have been covered, but none have been taught. What went wrong? We've all been there and done that. What does a teacher do to make sure this doesn't happen again?

A mini-lesson is just that—mini! The time limit for a mini-lesson is 15 minutes. That's not enough time to tell students everything about any subject! The teacher must begin by selecting a teaching objective for the mini-lesson. Think of this as having tunnel vision. The teacher is laser-focused and able to see the goal that has been chosen at the other end of the tunnel. Nothing should be able to deter him or her from teaching only that objective. Meanwhile, the teacher continues to observe and note the actions and reactions of students, and those become teaching points for another day.

How does a teacher determine what the teaching point needs to be? At the beginning of the year, most mini-lessons should be procedural, especially if the Workshop method is new to the students. The teacher will want to spend approximately thirty days establishing routines and building students' confidence in themselves as writers. After that time, the main focus of the mini-lessons will be developing the author's craft. Occasionally, mini-lessons will also focus on writer's conventions. Procedural mini-lessons will be revisited as necessary to ensure that the Workshop runs smoothly.

An observant teacher will notice when several students display a need for specific instruction. If just one or two students need this instruction, the topic can be addressed in a conference. If several students need the instruction, a mini-lesson is warranted. Often, when a teacher observes students struggling with the same instructional issue, this can become a mini-lesson the next day. The teacher should keep in mind that there are state and district grade-level expectations that need to be accommodated. Mini-lessons should be based on these expectations, as well as the developmental and instructional needs of the students.

At the end of this chapter, you will find suggestions for mini-lessons for the first thirty days of Writer's Workshop. There is a section for Kindergarten because the writing process will be new to the majority of these students. There is a section for Grades 1 and 2 and another for Grades 3–6. On the following page, you will find a mini-lesson planning form. You will also see a few appropriate ideas for craft and convention mini-lessons for Kindergarten, Grades 1 and 2, and Grades 3–6.

Suggestions for Mini-Lessons

	Author's Craft	Writing Conventions
Kindergarten	Matching words with picture Focusing on one topic Adding details Sequence Organization	Difference between a letter and a word Where to start writing Using capital letters Using periods Writing the sounds they hear
Grades 1–2	Writer's voice Literary elements Fiction vs. nonfiction Writing a strong lead Writing a strong ending Character development	Capital letters Ending punctuation Commas Run-on sentences Quotation marks Complete sentences
Grades 3–6	Using strong verbs Writer's voice Introducing genres Cutting unnecessary information Imagery Dialogue Text features and structures	Writing paragraphs Varying sentence length Commas Run-on sentences Quotation marks Subject/verb agreement Irregular nouns and verbs

Mini-Lesson Planning Form

Skill/Focus	
Book for Modeling	
Possible Student Work to Use as a Model	
Notes	

Mini-Lessons:
The First 30 Days of Writer's Workshop in Kindergarten

30 Days of Instruction

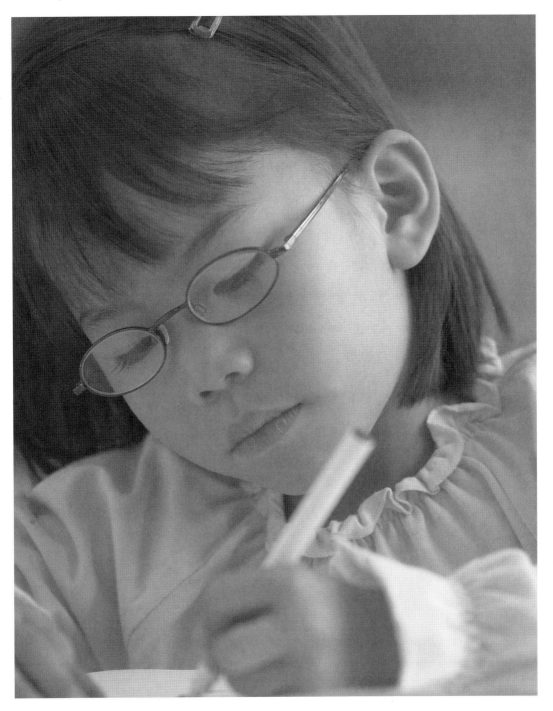

Teacher's Note

The first week of lessons will be for the entire workshop time. There will be no independent write for this week. This week will focus on building oral language and developing the joy of writing.

DAY 1 – Getting Ready for Writer's Workshop
Whole-Group Instruction and Oral Language Development

Purpose

- Encourage smooth transitions when coming and going to whole-group instruction.
- Show students where and how to sit during whole-group instruction.
- Begin oral language development by reading literature and modeling making connections and storytelling. (Teacher will need some objects reflecting a memory to use during the lesson—such as photos, mementos, etc.)

Teaching Points

- Show students the area where whole-group instruction will occur, and model how you want students to sit when they come to that area. You may want to assign students a place on the carpet so there won't be competition to sit in a certain place.

- Explain and model your signal (i.e. bell, clap, click, calling table groups, etc.) for transitioning students to whole-group instruction.

- Model the procedure for moving to the whole-group area. Then give students the opportunity to practice the procedure and how to sit quietly and attentively.

- **Say:** *When we move to the whole-group area, it will be a time to learn about writing.*

- **Say:** *We will begin Writer's Workshop the same way every day.*

- **Say:** *I have a special book that I want to share with you. The title is* **Something from Nothing** *by Phoebe Gilman (or any other book that deals with recording thoughts on paper).*

- Read the book to the students stopping a couple of times to think aloud and to model making connections.

- **Say:** *This book made me think about all of the stories in my head, even though I have nothing in my hand. For example, I think about the time (teacher will tell a story of their childhood). Here is a photo of me . . . Here is a memento from the trip . . .*

- Acknowledge any hands that may go up and reinforce the fact that they have made connections.

- **Say:** *Does this make you think of anything that happened to you?*
  Would someone like to share a story they remember?

- Allow students to tell stories. If any of their stories remind the teacher of a different memory, model the idea of being able to use what others say as a reminder of another story. Continue until the end of the workshop time.

- **Say:** *Many of you told wonderful stories today. Was it fun to hear your memories? Did you enjoy hearing my memories? Remember, we all have memories and stories to tell.*

- Review and model your signal (i.e. bell, clap, click, walking fingers, calling table groups, workstation groups, etc.) for leaving whole-group instruction.

- Use the signal and invite students to go back to their seats.

Encourage smooth transitions when coming and going to whole-group instruction.

DAY 2 – Getting Ready for Writer's Workshop
Good Listening Habits and Oral Language Development

Purpose

• Develop good listening habits.
• Introduce and Practice "Turn and Talk."
• Continue with oral language development.

Teaching Points

• Review and practice coming to the whole-group meeting area.

• **Say:** *There will be times when you all will want to share your thoughts. Today we are going to learn a way to do that called "Turn and Talk." When I invite you to turn and talk, you will sit knee to knee and look at your partner to take turns sharing an idea.*

• Teachers may want to assign students a partner they are sitting beside and can work with so the same partner is available each time.

• Choose a student to be your partner and model what it looks like to turn and talk.

• Invite the students to practice turning and talking. Invite them to talk about why it's important to listen to you partner. Make sure they understand they should be knee to knee and looking at their partner.

• After asking students to again focus on the teacher, discuss why it's important to have good listening habits including appropriate noise levels.

• **Say:** *Today I have another special book to share with you. The title is* **Wolf!** *by Becky Bloom (or any other book that models storytelling).*

• The teacher models making connections with this book and telling another memory.

• **Say:** *I see that many of you have stories you would like to share. Since I know that all of you would like a turn, let's practice our new strategy. Turn and talk to your partner.*

• The teacher will want to listen to the students tell their stories to each other. Pay special attention to good stories that some of the reluctant students have told.

• **Say:** *While listening to the partners, I heard (name) tell a very good story. (Name), will you share your story with the class?*

• Dismiss class practicing signals and behavior when returning to seats or moving on to write independently.

DAY 3 – Getting Ready for Writer's Workshop
Good Listening Habits and Oral Language Development

Purpose

- Develop good listening habits.
- Practice "Turn and Talk."
- Continue with oral language development.

Teaching Points

- Review and practice coming to the whole-group meeting area.

- **Say:** *There will be many times during Writer's Workshop when you listen to a speaker. You may be asked to listen to your teacher when they are talking with you. You may be asked to listen to a friend and you may want your friend to listen to you. When you listen to a speaker, what are some of the important things to remember?*

- Brainstorm and create an anchor chart listing characteristics of a good listener using modeled writing. Title the chart Characteristics of a Good Listener.

- **Say:** *Today I'd like to share a story titled **Martha Speaks** by Susan Meddaugh (or another story about animals). Remember to be a good listener as I read the story to you.*

- Read the story to the students and model telling a story you have about animals.

- Remind students of the procedures of turning and talking to a partner.

- **Say:** *I see that many of you have animal stories you would like to share. Since I know that all of you would like a turn, let's practice turning and talking to your partner.*

- The teacher will want to listen to the students tell their stories to each other. Pay special attention to good stories that some of the reluctant students have told.

- **Say:** *While listening to the partners, I heard (name) tell a very good story. (Name), will you share your story with the class?*

- **Ask:** *As we were working on our anchor chart, what did you do today that made you a good listener? What could you do tomorrow to make yourself a better listener? Is there anything you would like to add to our chart?*

- Dismiss class practicing signals and behavior when returning to seats or moving on to write independently.

Characteristics of
a Good Listener

1. Look at the speaker.

2. Sit quietly. Shhh.

3. Keep my hands in my lap.

DAY 4 – Getting Ready for Writer's Workshop
Creating a Topic List of Writing Ideas and Oral Language Development

Purpose

- Practice good listening habits.
- Create a list of possible writing topics.
- Continue with oral language development.

Teaching Points

- Review and practice coming to the whole-group meeting area.

- **Say:** *Today I'd like to share another story. This story is titled **Wilfrid Gordon McDonald Partridge** by Mem Fox (or **All the Places to Love** by Patricia MacLachlan). Remember to be a good listener as I read the story to you.*

- Read the story to the students and model telling a story you have about any connection you can make to the book.

- Remind students of the procedures of turning and talking to a partner.

- **Say:** *I see that many of you have many stories you would like to share. Since I know that all of you would like a turn, let's practice turning and talking to your partner.*

- Listen to the students tell their stories to one another. Pay special attention to good stories that some of the reluctant students have told.

- **Say:** *While I was listening to (name's) story, it reminded me of another story that I have.*

- Tell the story to the students and then **say:** *I have told so many stories and I want to make a list of them. I think I should just write down a few words to help me remember the topic of my stories. For example, I just told you a story about (my grandmother's quilt). I think I should just write down "grandmother's quilt" on my list.*

- Model writing *I can write about . . .* at the top of a piece of chart paper. Write a #1 and put "grandmother's quilt" after the number. Draw a small picture of a quilt beside the words to help students remember what the topic was.

- **Say:** *Help me remember what some of my stories were about.*

- As students brainstorm the stories that you told, list them on your chart and draw small pictures beside the words to help students remember the stories.

- **Say:** *I loved telling these stories, but I would like to tell the whole story in writing or with pictures. You may want to write or draw about some of your stories, too!*

- Dismiss class practicing signals and behavior when returning to seats or moving on to write independently.

I can write about . . .

1. grandmother's quilt

DAY 5 – Getting Ready for Writer's Workshop
Creating a Topic List of Writing Ideas and Oral Language Development

Purpose

- Practice good listening habits.
- Create a list of possible writing topics.
- Continue with oral language development.

Teaching Points

- Review and practice coming to the whole-group meeting area.

- **Say:** *Today I'd like to share another story. This story is titled* **Arthur Writes a Story** *by Marc Brown* (or another story that centers around writing). *Remember to be a good listener as I read the story to you.*

- Read the story to the students and model telling a story you have about any connection you can make to the book.

- **Say:** *I see that many of you have many stories you would like to share. Since I know that all of you would like a turn, let's practice turning and talking to your partner.*

- The teacher will want to listen to the students tell their stories to one another and allow one or two students to share their stories with the whole group.

- **Say:** *All of you have shared many stories with your partner or with the class. Yesterday I made a list of the stories that I have told, and I would like you to be able to list your stories, too. Remember that you have told stories about memories, your family, animals, etc.* (Recap subjects that you have discussed.)

- Display the *I can write about . . .* list that you wrote during Day 4 and remind students how they helped you compile your list. Model using a large piece of manila paper folded into sixths.

- **Say:** *Since the first story on my list is about a quilt, I'll draw a quilt in this first square. Since my next story was about my pet, I'll draw a picture of a dog* (or whatever animal your story was about . . .) *in the next square.* Keep modeling until students understand.

- **Say:** *Now think about all of the stories that you have told during this week. We will now have time for you to draw a quick picture of some of the stories that you can tell.*

- Distribute large pieces of manila paper folded into sixths, and ask students to return to their seats to compose their lists by drawing a picture in each square that represents a story they told. Support students who are struggling to remember some of the stories that they have told.

Teacher's Note

You may have to explain the difference between a quick sketch used to remind students of a main idea and a detailed picture used to 'tell a story' or 'talk about text.'

Teacher's Note

If some of your students are developmentally ready to write words, invite then to label their pictures with a word or words about the story.

- After 15–20 minutes, use your signal to call students back to the whole-group area. Ask them to bring their papers with them.

- **Say:** *You have each worked very hard and drawn a quick picture about many of the stories that you have told. Some of you may not have finished your list, but you will have time tomorrow to add to it. Remember that this list will never be finished. You can always add to it whenever you remember a good story or have something that you would like to tell or to write.*

- Dismiss students using your signal.

DAY 6 – Writer's Workshop Procedures
Using and Storing Writing Folders

Purpose

- Guide students in the proper use and care of their writing folders.
- Help students understand where their folders are stored and how to return them to the storage place.

Teaching Points

- Use your signal to call students to the whole-group meeting area.

- Hold up a folder that you have predetermined each student will use as their writing folder. (Usually these folders are uniform in appearance. They are the same color and type for easy identification as a writing folder.)

- **Say:** *You will each have a folder that looks like this. This is your writing folder. You will want to put your name on your folder* (if it is not already labeled). *You will use your folder to store all of your writing and other resources writers use. Your topic list will go inside this folder. When we come back for our mini-lesson, you will want to bring your folder with you. We will store our folders* (in a predetermined place) *and return them when Writer's Workshop is over.*

- Model a folder you have assembled with your own writing. Show that your name is on the front of your folder and that you have included pieces of your writing that are "in progress" or "completed." You may want to show that you have stapled your topic sheet on the inside cover.

- **Say:** *Your writing folder is your tool to help you organize your writing and keep your writing from getting lost. It will be one of your most important resources when you write. You will want to keep it with you during Writer's Workshop.*

- **Say:** *We keep our writing folders in the same place each day. It is very important to get and return our folders carefully. We keep them neat and don't bend or tear them. We take care of them since we use them every day.* (Model the storage place and how the folders should look before and after the students have returned their folders to the proper place.)

- **Say:** *Let's practice how to get and replace our folders in a neat, orderly manner.*

- Give each student their writing folder and allow them to practice putting the folder in the storage place.

- Model for the students how to follow the procedure (calling rows, tables, students, etc.) when you are ready to end Writer's Workshop. Practice until the students are able to retrieve and store folders correctly and quietly.

Teacher's Note

At this time of year, you may want to have the folders already labeled with the students' names.

Teacher's Note

For today's lesson only, the writing time is included in this lesson so that students will be prepared for Day 7.

- **Writing Time:** Distribute the topic list that they compiled on Day 5. Ask students to return to their seats. Invite them to place their name on the front of the folder if you have not chosen to do that beforehand and then add to their topic lists. As students are working, circulate and show students how they can follow the folds of their manila paper and store it in a pocket of their folder after they finish using it.

DAY 7 – Writer's Workshop
Choosing the Writing Topic

Purpose

• Guide students in the process of choosing a topic for writing from their list.

Teaching Points

• Use your signal to call students to the whole-group meeting area.

• The teacher should have his or her own topic list that was compiled with the students available to use for this mini-lesson.

• The students need to have their writing folder with them.

• **Say:** *These are all stories that I could tell and write. This one is one of my favorite stories. I will put a star beside this topic to remind me that I want to write about this first. Now look at your topic list. Decide on your favorite topic. Now turn to your partner and tell the whole story.*

• **Say:** *When you hear the signal, please take your writing folder and go back to your seat to write or draw what you told your partner.*

• Distribute unlined paper to the students. This can be another sheet of manila paper that is not folded. If students are developmentally drawing pictures, this picture should contain much more detail that the sketch on their "topic list" of pictures.

• Dismiss students from the mini-lesson using your signal.

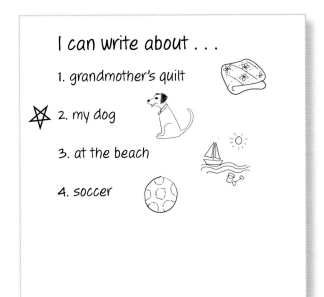

DAY 8 – Concept of Writer's Workshop

Purpose

- Introduce concept of Writer's Workshop to students.
- Clarify the purpose of Writer's Workshop.

Teaching Points

- Use your signal to call students to the whole-group meeting area.

- **Say:** *Today we will be talking about Writer's Workshop and what it is.*

- Draw a blank three-column chart. As you explain and discuss the components (mini-lesson, independent writing time, and sharing time) of Writer's Workshop, you will complete the chart.

- Begin by explaining the mini-lesson. Write "Mini-Lesson" (it may be helpful to draw an icon beside the words to help the students remember what the words say) at the top of the first column.

- **Say:** *We have been learning about how we come together as a whole group to learn more about writing. This is one part of Writer's Workshop.*

- Write or draw one or two ideas in the Mini-Lesson column.

- Write "Writing Time" (it may be helpful to draw an icon beside the words to help the students remember what the words say) at the top of the second column. Explain that students will be doing different things during writing time. Explain that most of their writing time will be spent writing and using the writing process. Explain that the students will be learning about the writing process during their mini-lessons.

- Write or draw one or two ideas in the Writing Time column.

- **Say:** *After our mini-lesson, we will use what we learn about writing to write stories or pieces of writing that interests us. We will use the writing process when we write, so each of us may be at different places in the writing process.*

- Write "Sharing Time" (it may be helpful to draw an icon beside the words to help the students remember what the words say) at the top of the third column. Explain the students will have an opportunity to share what they have written with other students in the class. Explain that they will also hear what others have written.

- Write or draw one or two ideas in the Sharing Time column.

- **Say:** *There will be times to share with the group or a partner about things you have written. You may get help from your friends about a writing problem, read an especially interesting part of your writing to a friend, or listen to a friend's writing as they read to you.*

- Ask students to share ideas about how Writer's Workshop will help them become better writers.

- Dismiss students from the mini-lesson using signals.

- Students will write independently at the end of each day's mini-lesson.

Writer's Workshop

Mini-Lesson	Writing Time	Sharing Time
1. Learn about writing.	1. Write	1. Listen to others share their writing.
2. Listen to the teacher.	2. Draw	

Teacher's Note

When working with younger students, we found it helpful to start with minimal tools at the writing table such as unlined pieces of paper (different types, colors, and sizes) and pencils, markers, and crayons. As the other tools were needed, we introduced them one at a time.

DAY 9 – Writer's Workshop Procedures
Using and Storing Writing Tools

Purpose

- Introduce students to storage places for writing tools.
- Guide students in the proper use and storage of materials.

Teaching Points

- Use your signal to call students to the whole-group meeting area.

- Tell your students that today you are going to tell them about a place in your room where they will find many things they will need as writers. Invite your class to come with you to the writing table or to the location in the classroom where materials will be stored. Tell your students that these are resources that they will need when writing books. (Have several different tools there to share with the students. Suggestions: loose leaf notebook paper, unlined paper, construction paper, stapler, tape, hole punch, rulers, scissors, pens for editing, sharpened pencils, markers, dictionaries, thesauri, etc.) Take the time to talk about each item, emphasizing that these are tools, not toys. Help students understand that it will be their responsibility to use them wisely and for the correct purpose.

- **Say:** *When you need a piece of paper or something to write or draw with, you will be able to come to our writing table to get what you need.*

- Invite the students to return to the whole-group meeting area and find their seat. Debrief the location of the writing tools and their use. Create an anchor chart titled "Tools Students Use When Writing." Invite the students to help list the tools and note how each tool is used. Post the anchor chart over the writing table or in the writing area. You may want to add icons as the students talk about the materials you have listed. You may also want to place limits such as one piece of paper at a time, etc.

- Dismiss students from the mini-lesson using signals.

- Students will write independently at the end of each day's mini-lesson.

Tools Students Use When Writing

1. notebook paper
2. unlined paper
3. pencils/pens
4. stapler

. . .

DAY 10 – Writer's Workshop Procedures
Creating an Effective Atmosphere for Writers

Purpose

- Guide students in developing rules for Writer's Workshop.
- Help students understand what Writer's Workshop looks like and sounds like.

Teaching Points

- Call students to the whole-group meeting area using your practiced signal.

- Using the anchor charts, review with students what makes a good listener and what Writer's Workshop is.

- **Say:** *We know that during Writer's Workshop we learn about writing. There are ways that we can work together to make our classroom a better place to write. Today we are going to brainstorm what we can do to make our classroom a place where we can work and write together.*

- Introduce a two-column T-Chart that will help students clarify what Writer's Workshop looks like and sounds like. Title the two columns "Looks Like" (draw a picture of an eye beside the words) and "Sounds Like" (draw a picture of an ear beside the words). This is a fluid chart that you will add to during the year as your Workshop develops.

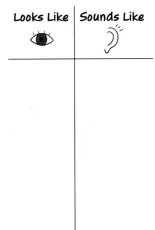

- **Say:** *Use only your eyes. What would you see if you walked into our room during Writer's Workshop?* (i.e. students sitting on the floor in whole group for the mini-lesson, students talking with the teacher, students talking and writing with one another, students writing independently, students sharing, etc.)

- Record students' ideas on the T-Chart under the column "Looks Like" using words and pictures.

- **Say:** *Use only your ears. What would you hear if you walked into our room during Writer's Workshop?* (i.e. students using tools, pencils scratching, students moving around the room quietly, students quietly sharing with partners and/or a teacher, the teacher teaching a mini-lesson, etc.)

- Record students' ideas on the T-Chart under the column "Sounds Like" using words and pictures.

- Use the anchor charts as resources to revisit when you face problematic situations during your Workshop.

- Dismiss students from the mini-lesson using your signal.

- Students will write independently at the end of each day's mini-lesson.

DAY 11 – Writer's Workshop Procedures
Appropriate Behavior

Purpose

• Discuss behavior that is appropriate and conducive to writing.

Teaching Points

• Use your signal to call students to the whole-group meeting area.

• **Say:** *When I am writing, I need to be able to think about my good ideas and put those ideas in writing. I can't write well if someone is bothering me. What helps you to do your best thinking and writing? What helps Writer's Workshop run smoothly?*

• Brainstorm a list of appropriate behaviors and post them on a chart entitled "Writer's Workshop Rules." These rules could include:
  —You may participate in the writing process during the entire time.
  —You may not disturb others.
  —You may sit in a comfortable place.
  —Listen when asked.
  —Be ready to share when asked.
  —Make sure you get and replace your writing folder at the proper time, etc.
Use pictures to make sure the meaning of the words is clear to students.

• **Say:** *I will place our rules on the wall so that we can refer to them at any time. In addition, if we think of other rules that we need to add, we can do that.*

• **Say:** *Be sure that you follow our workshop rules as you write today and every day.*

• Dismiss students using your signal.

Writer's Workshop Rules

• You may not disturb others.

• You may sit in a comfortable place.

• Listen when asked.

• Be ready to share when asked.

DAY 12 – Writer's Workshop Procedures
Where to Sit

Purpose

- Guide students in sitting in the location that is most conducive to writing.
- Help students understand where and when they might move to a new location to write.

Teaching Points

- Use your signal to call students to the whole-group meeting area.

- Model sitting at your desk to write something or at different places in the room.

- **Say:** *Is there only one place in the classroom that you could write? What other places do you think would make good writing spots?*

- Brainstorm a list of places that students have seen you engaged in writing.

- **Say:** *You have noticed that there are many places in this classroom that I can write, and there are reasons why I might need to move to another location. As writers, you might be very comfortable writing at your desk, but there may be other places in this classroom that you might also be able to write. Let's create a chart to help us remember good places to write.*

- Create a web on chart paper that students can use as an anchor chart. Note any appropriate places that children might be able to sit during writing time, drawing a picture of those places or drawing map of the room with a star on those places (a table in the classroom, a corner that is away from others, a desk beside another student while conferring, on the floor, etc.).

- **Say:** *You can move to any place in the classroom that is comfortable and helps you to stay focused while you are writing. Remember that this must be a place where you are not disturbing others while they are writing.*

- **Say:** *Now let's practice finding a good place to write as we continue with Writer's Workshop.*

- Dismiss students using your signal.

Teacher's Note

It will be important to post a visual that will help students reflect on the writing process. The visual should be in a spot in the room that is accessible and continuously available for reference. (See figure below for a suggested format.)

DAY 13 – Introduce the Writing Process

Purpose

- Review the prewriting piece of Writer's Workshop.
- Create an anchor chart with the writing process cycle.

Teaching Points

- Call students to the whole-group meeting area using your practiced signal.

- **Say:** *Today we're going to begin learning about the process good writers use when they are writing a story or any piece of writing. Most authors follow this cycle or one very similar to it every time they create a piece of writing. Since we're authors too, we want to learn how this cycle, or writing process, will help us be better writers. We have been writing stories and placing them in our writing folders. Now we will learn what we can do next.*

- Show students the list of stories that you made on Day 5. Add another topic to your list that concerns something that happened at school. The story should be one that students can contribute thoughts and ideas. Tell them that tomorrow they will help you write that story.

- **Say:** *Be thinking about ideas for the story that we will write tomorrow.*

- Dismiss class from the mini-lesson using practiced signals and behavior.

- Students will write independently at the end of each day's mini-lesson.

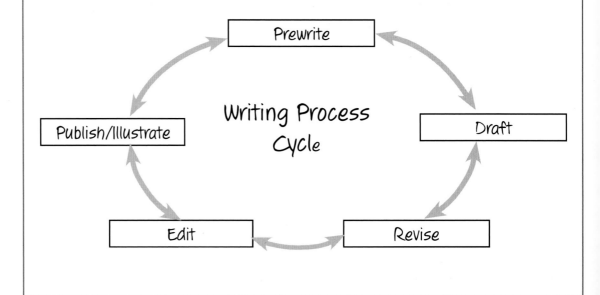

DAY 14 – Continue Prewriting Using a Web

Purpose

- Explain to students the importance of prewriting.
- Create a story web.

Teaching Points

- Call students to the whole-group meeting area using your practiced signal.

- Revisit the brainstorming process and remind students about the new idea that they will all help to write.

- **Say:** *When good writers begin a story or any writing, they use a tool to help them record their ideas so they can think about their story in an organized way. One of the tools some writers choose to use is a web. Today, we're going to use the idea we decided on yesterday to create a web for our story.*

- On a piece of chart paper, draw a circle in the center with the idea students chose to write about written in the center of the circle. Around that idea, write or draw the details as students brainstorm creating a web that will drive the direction of the story or event. Be sure to guide students into including the literary elements of character, setting, problem, and solution. (See example below.)

- Dismiss class from the mini-lesson using practiced signals and behavior.

- Students will write independently at the end of each day's mini-lesson.

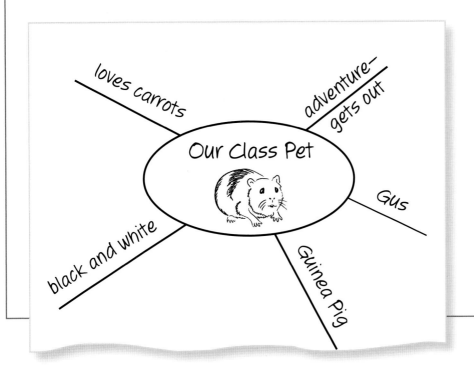

DAY 15 – Continue Prewriting

Purpose

• Create an anchor chart showing different kinds of prewriting.

Teaching Points

• Call students to the whole-group meeting area using your practiced signal.

• **Say:** *We have been using a web to do our prewriting for our story. As you practice writing, you may choose other ways to prewrite. Today we are going to create an anchor chart with different ideas about prewriting. The chart may help you choose a way to prewrite that will help you organize ideas for a piece of writing.*

• Using a piece of chart paper, title the anchor chart "Prewriting." Invite your students to give ideas of different ways to prewrite. (make lists, draw pictures, brainstorm, use graphic organizers, etc.)

• **Say:** *After you have finished your prewriting, remember to store that paper in your writing folders so you have it when you begin writing your story.*

• Dismiss class from the mini-lesson using practiced signals and behavior.

• Students will write independently at the end of each day's mini-lesson.

Prewriting

1. Draw pictures

2. Make a list

3. Brainstorm

DAY 16 – Continue Prewriting

Purpose

- Review the prewriting step of the writing.
- Know that each story has a beginning, middle, and end.
- Create an anchor chart showing the characteristics of a beginning, middle, and end of a story.

Teaching Points

- Make sure you have the writing process anchor chart posted in a place where you can easily refer to the writing process cycle. Call attention to the writing process cycle and review the process of prewriting. Talk with your class about the next step in the process—rough draft.

- **Say:** *When a writer is ready to begin writing the rough draft, it is important to look over the prewriting and think about where to start writing. Every story has a beginning. In the beginning, an author may put the character and setting.*

- Use the class prewriting from Day 13 and identify the character and setting. (At this developmental age, it may be useful to identify the elements of the chart pertinent to the beginning of the story with a "B" or "1".)

- **Say:** *Every story has a middle. In the middle, a writer tells what in happening in the story. This may sound like a problem in the story.*

- Use the class prewriting to identify the points that may be in the middle of the story. (At this developmental age, it may be useful to identify the elements of the chart pertinent to the middle of the story with an "M" or "2".)

- **Say:** *Every story has an ending. In the end, a writer could tell how a problem is solved.*

- Use the class prewriting to identify the points that could be in the ending of the story. (At this developmental age, it may be useful to identify the elements of the chart pertinent to the ending of the story with an "E" or "3".)

- **Say:** *When we start writing our story, it will be important to use our prewriting to help us make sure we don't leave any part of our story out.*

- Using chart paper, create a three-column T-Chart. Title the first column "Beginning," the second column "Middle," and the third column "End." Invite the class to contribute ideas of what a writer could put in the beginning of a story (details describing a character[s], details describing the setting, etc.), in the middle of a story (details describing a problem, events leading up to a problem, how a character reacts to the problem, etc.), and at the end of a story (details describing how a problem is solved, how a character feels about the solutions, how the solution affects the character, etc.).

Teacher's Note

It would be helpful to connect the symbols used on the prewrite web for beginning, middle, and end with this anchor chart.

- Post the anchor chart where students can use it for a reference to write the rough draft of the story.

- Dismiss class from the mini-lesson using practiced signals and behavior.

- Students will write independently at the end of each day's mini-lesson.

B Beginning	M Middle	E End
Describe character	Describe problem	Describe solution
example: Characters: Susan Joe Susan is smart.		
Describe setting example: a school	Events leading to a problem	Describe characters feelings about solution

Day 17 – Begin Rough Draft Step of Writing Process Cycle

Purpose

- Review the Beginning, Middle, and End Anchor Chart.
- Understand that the rough draft is written on every other line.
- Begin writing the rough draft of your class story.

Teaching Points

- Call students to the whole-group meeting area using your practiced signal.

- It is important to have the writing process posted in a place where you can easily refer to the writing process cycle. Call attention to the writing process cycle and review the process of prewriting. Talk with the class about the next step in the process—rough draft.

- **Say:** *When a writer is ready to start writing a rough draft, the first thing that an author does is look at the prewriting to see where he or she wants to start. The last time we met, we identified the points that we could put at the beginning of our rough draft.*

- **Say:** *When an author is writing the rough draft, it is important that his or her attention is on putting thoughts on paper. You will probably make some spelling errors, grammar errors, or have story elements you will eventually want to change. The most important thing about a rough draft is that you spend your time writing and putting your ideas on paper.*

- **Say:** *It is also important to remember that we will write on every other line. Writers do this because there will come a time when they will need that extra line to fix up the story.*

- Using a piece of chart paper, begin the process of writing the rough draft of your class story using modeled and shared writing. (Be sure that you skip lines on the paper.) Invite the class to contribute ideas for the story using the prewriting web and chart as a guide.

- Begin writing the rough draft, inviting students to contribute sentences and ideas for the beginning of the class story. Continue with this process until your mini-lesson time is up. Tell the students that you will continue with the story tomorrow. You will use your mini-lesson time for the next couple of days until the rough draft for your story is complete.

- Dismiss class from the mini-lesson using practiced signals and behavior.

- Students will write independently at the end of each day's mini-lesson.

Teacher's Note

It's important to remember that students at this age are at different developmental writing stages. Some of the students will only be drawing pictures when writing independently while others will be writing in the scribble stage and others will be using some letters and words. Most experts believe that scribing is not appropriate for students in these various stages, but accepting whatever writing they do is very important.

Teacher's Note

You will want to encourage your students to reread often. They need to make sure that their writing makes sense and that their message conveys what they intended.

DAYS 18–19 – Continue Writing Process Cycle
Rough Draft

Purpose

• Continue using the writing process cycle (rough draft) to create a class story emphasizing a beginning, middle, and end to the story.

Teaching Points

• Call students to the whole-group meeting area using your practiced signal.

• **Say:** *Today we will continue writing the rough draft of our story. Who knows what part of our story we are ready to draft? How do you know?* (By looking at our prewriting and looking at the points we want to write about.)

• Reread the rough draft of what has been written so far. Continue writing the rough draft using modeled and shared writing until your mini-lesson time is over. Make sure that the ideas you are recording are stated simply. Too much text will be overwhelming for students at this stage of development.

• You will use your mini-lesson time for a couple of days to complete the rough draft.

• Dismiss class from the mini-lesson using practiced signals and behavior.

• Students will write independently at the end of each day's mini-lesson.

DAY 20 – Completing the Rough Draft

Purpose

• Create an anchor chart entitled "Rough Draft."

Teaching Points

• Call students to the whole-group meeting area using your practiced signal.

• **Say:** *We have been writing the rough draft of our story. Let's create an anchor chart about the important points of a rough draft.*

• Using a piece of chart paper, title the anchor chart "Rough Draft." Use an icon or picture that you have chosen to indicate this stage of writing. Invite the students to contribute ideas about writing a rough draft and record their thoughts using words and pictures. (Write many sentences; follow your prewriting plan; write all of your story; make sure you write a beginning, middle, and end in your story; make sure you have characters, setting, problem and solution; correctly spell words that you know; put down what you know about words that you don't know, etc.)

• Post the rough draft anchor chart beside the prewriting anchor chart. This assures availability to the students when working their way through the writing process cycle.

• Dismiss class from the mini-lesson using practiced signals and behavior.

• Students will write independently at the end of each day's mini-lesson.

Rough Draft

1. Write sentences.

2. Follow prewrite.

DAY 21 – Introduce Revising
Using a Caret

Purpose

• Introduce students to the revising step of the writing process cycle.
• Use completed class story to model revising concept.
• Model the use of a caret as a revision tool used to insert one or two words.

Teaching Points

• Call students to the whole-group meeting area using your practiced signal.

• **Say:** *Do you remember what a good reader does after they finish reading? That's right. They go back and think about their reading. A good writer does about the same thing. After an author has written the rough draft, a good writer goes back over their writing and thinks about how their story sounds. There are many things to think about. An author may think about the character, setting, problem, and solution. They may think about using describing words, adding sentences to make their writing clearer, or adding whole chunks to a story to make it more exciting or easier for their audience to read. Today we're going to look at one way to revise your writing.*

• Reread the story that the class wrote together. While you read, think aloud to model the process of adding adjectives to provide description.

• **Say:** *I'm reading this sentence. It says that . . .* (For example: "It says that the bear ran after the rabbit. I ask myself what kind of bear it was. Was it a baby bear? Was it a big bear? Was it fat? Was it hungry?") *I think that we could add a word to this sentence to make it more interesting. We could also help the reader visualize the . . . What word do you think we could add to this sentence? Could we add more than one? Where else could we add a word?*

• Continue through the story finding appropriate places to use the caret. Then write an adjective above the caret on the blank line that is formed as lines are skipped during writing. Use some discretion when choosing words so that there are only one or two examples.

• **Say:** *When you are ready to make revisions to your story, you may want to try using a caret if you just need to add one or two words. You can also think about your picture. You can decide if you want to add one or two details to your picture to make it tell more about the story you told.*

• Dismiss class from the mini-lesson using practiced signals and behavior.

• Students will write independently at the end of each day's mini-lesson.

The ^silly^ guinea pig
saw a ^lunch^ ticket.

DAY 22 – Continue Revising
Using Spider Legs

Purpose

- Model the use of a spider leg as a revision tool used when adding one or two sentences to a rough draft.

Teaching Points

- Call students to the whole-group meeting area using your practiced signal.

- **Say:** *The step of the writing process that we've been learning about is revising. This step is difficult for some writers because it's hard to change what they have written. Remember that, when we make revisions, we are making our writing more interesting, more accurate, and more complete. There are times when we revise that we may need to add more than a word to our writing. We many want to add a sentence. We're going to use a tool called a spider leg.*

- Read through the class story to find a place where another sentence could be added for clarity or detail.

- Model cutting a strip of writing paper and taping it on the draft where you want to add the sentence.

- **Say:** *Now you're ready to write your sentence on this strip of paper. When you read the story, read this sentence with the rest of your story.*

- Continue modeling using the spider leg revision tool by inviting the class to find another place where a sentence could be added to the rough draft that was written in class on Days 17–19.

- **Say:** *When you are ready to make revisions to your story, you may want to try using this tool. The strips are already cut. You can find them back on the writing table* (or any place that would be convenient for students).

- Dismiss class from the mini-lesson using practiced signals and behavior.

- Students will write independently at the end of each day's mini-lesson.

The
silly
guinea pig

saw a
lunch
ticket.

He tore it up.

He wanted it

for his nest.

DAY 23 – Continue Revising
Review Using Carets and Spider Legs

Purpose

• Create an anchor chart for revising.

Teaching Points

• Call students to the whole-group meeting area using your practiced signal.

• **Say:** *We have learned a couple of ways to revise our writing. Today we will create an anchor chart titled "Revising."*

• Invite the students to give ideas about revising and what methods they could use to revise. (Carets are used when adding one or two words, Spider Legs are used when adding sentences, response groups are used to help an author revise, etc.) As the students share their ideas, record the words with pictures or symbols to help the students understand the text.

• Post the anchor chart with the Prewrite and Rough Draft anchor charts. Remind the students to use these charts as a resource as they move through the writing process cycle.

• Dismiss class from the mini-lesson using practiced signals and behavior.

• Students will write independently at the end of each day's mini-lesson.

Revising

1. Carets for 1 word

2. Spider legs for a sentence

DAY 24 – Introduce Response Groups

Purpose

- Explain what a response group is.
- Model what a response group looks like and sounds like.

Teaching Points

- Call students to the whole-group meeting area using your practiced signal.

- **Say:** *When you are ready to begin the revisions on your writing, it helps to have someone listen to your writing or listen to your story about your picture and give you ideas. Today we are going to use a response group to help us revise. A response group is a group of three sitting knee to knee and eye to eye. The purpose to give an author a place to read the story and talk with an audience about the story.*

- Invite a group of three students to sit on the floor in a triangle. They are close enough that a soft voice can be heard and used, but not close enough to touch. Inform the class that the person who asks for a response group is the author of a piece of writing. They then choose two people to join them in the group. Choose one of the group to act as the author. You may want that student to read a piece of their own writing or tell about a picture they've drawn, or use the class story.

- Model by having the author read the story and by having the other two students respond to the reading. Remind the students that respect and kindness are always used when participating in a response group. If students have difficulty with this, you might want to become one of the "students" in the group in order to model an appropriate response.

- **Say:** *You may want to call a response group when you are ready to revise. Only two response groups may be held at one time. This is the place where you may have your response groups.*

- Dismiss class from the mini-lesson using practiced signals and behavior.

- Students will write independently at the end of each day's mini-lesson.

Teacher's Note

If your students are not familiar with the process of listening and responding to another student's writing, it will be necessary to provide guidelines before attempting this. You may want to have a separate mini-lesson to create an anchor chart titled "Response Groups" with suggestions from the following list: Listen politely. Ask questions to help the author develop the story. Use positive comments. Make kind suggestions to help with detail or answer questions you may have.

Teacher's Note

Remember that you will see many developmental stages of writing at this age. It is important that each writer feels that his or her writing is valid and valuable.

Teacher's Note

We always try to find one period that needs to be placed and one capital that need to be placed at the beginning of a sentence in our class story. We try to intentionally leave these errors when we write the story.

Teacher's Note

Common editing marks are included on page 180. You will be the best judge as to the levels of mastery your students will have when identifying spelling, punctuation, and capitalization errors. You may want to create a chart for your students to use as a resource with the editing marks noted.

DAY 25 - Introduce Editing

Purpose

• Introduce students to editing.

Teaching Points

• Call students to the whole-group meeting area using your practiced signal.

• Point out the editing step in the writing process by referencing the writing process cycle.

• **Say:** *After authors have revised their writing, then they look at the next step in the writing process. This is the editing step. It is important that writing has no spelling, capitalization, or punctuation errors. The first step is for the author to look for mistakes by rereading. Then an author often asks someone to help them continue the process. You will do the same thing when you ask someone to be your editor. Your editor will help you read through your writing to look for errors. During the year, we will learn many new things about grammar, capitalization, punctuation, and spelling. You will be expected to use what we learn as you edit your own writing and the writing of others. Your editor will help you look for capitals and periods. He or she might help you write some words you are using if they know how to spell them or if they can help you find them on our word wall.*

• Edit your class story or a story that has at least one spelling error, one capitalization error, and one punctuation error. Invite students to correct errors they see as you read the story. Use three lines under a letter that needs to be capitalized and place a punctuation mark within a circle where it is missing.

• **Say:** *You may be ready to edit your writing. Remember to reread your writing to find and correct as many errors as possible before asking a classmate to be your editor.*

• Dismiss class from the mini-lesson using practiced signals and behavior.

• Students will write independently at the end of each day's mini-lesson.

DAY 26 – Editing, continued

Purpose

- Explain that conferring with the teacher is part of the editing step of the writing process.
- Make an anchor chart about what to do as they wait to confer with the teacher.

Teaching Points

- Call students to the whole-group meeting area using your practiced signal.

- Point out the editing step in the writing process by referencing the writing process cycle.

- **Say:** *After authors have edited their writing with a partner, they are almost ready to publish their writing.*

- Display the story that was written together on Days 17–19 and reread it with students. Refer to the Writing Process Cycle chart.

- **Say:** *Now that we are almost ready to publish our story, we need to confer with the teacher, who will be your editor-in-chief, the person in charge of publications. This is part of the editing process. I will be your editor-in-chief. When you get the editor-in-chief's approval, you may begin the publishing process.*

- Hold up a spiral or a loose-leaf notebook that is labeled "Conference with Teacher."

- **Say:** *You will sign your name in this notebook when you have revised, edited, and then reread your writing. When you sign, I may be busy working with other students, but this is your way of letting me know that you are almost ready to publish. I will get to you as soon as I can. In the meantime, you have choices about what you can do. You can begin to write something new. Since we know that Writer's Workshop is never finished, what other things could you do while you are waiting for a conference with me?*

- Create a web with "What to Do as I Wait for a Conference" in the center. Students might suggest: finish another piece of writing, edit with another student, be part of a response group, add to the topic list, begin a new draft, etc.

- **Say:** *There may be other times during the writing process that you need to confer with the editor-in-chief. I want you to know that you are welcome to sign the notebook at any time—if you are stuck or if you need help in any way.*

- Refer again to the Writing Process Cycle. Make it clear to students that they must revise, edit, and reread before they are ready to confer.

- Indicate where the notebook will be placed. It's a good idea to use yarn or a string to tie a pencil to the notebook.

- Dismiss class from the mini-lesson using practiced signals and behavior.

- Students will write independently at the end of each day's mini-lesson.

What to Do as I Wait for a Conference

- finish another piece of writing

- edit with another student

- be part of a response group

- add to the topic list

- prewrite

- begin a draft

etc.

DAY 27 – Conferring with the Teacher

Purpose

- Discuss the procedures of teacher/student conferences and their importance.

Teaching Points

- Call students to the whole-group meeting area using your practiced signal.

- Point out the editing step with students and review with them what they need to do during this step of the writing process.

- **Say:** *After authors have edited their writing with their other writers, then they need to talk to the editor-in-chief. We will review your writing once again to ensure that it is ready for publication. We will read your piece together, and then we might focus on one, or possibly two, items that would improve your writing. You might choose to make any changes to your writing during the conference, or you might decide to go back to your writing place to do your final work. You need to have the approval of the editor-in-chief before you begin to publish.*

- **Say:** *Let's review the writing process. If we have revised and edited our writing, we are almost ready to publish. What should we do now? Yes, we sign the conference notebook so that we can meet with the editor-in-chief. When the teacher is ready to confer, we bring our writing folder and our pencil to the conference table. We are prepared to read our writing with the editor-in-chief.*

- Model the conferring process by selecting a student to sit with you and read his or her story or tell about his or her picture. Tell something that you liked about the writing or picture, and be supportive of the student's efforts. Then select one teaching point or suggestion for this student. Ask the student what he or she thinks about your suggestion, and ask if he or she would like to make that change.

- **Say:** *After you have revised, edited, and reread your paper, you are ready to confer with the editor-in-chief. Some of you might be ready for this part of the editing process.*

- Dismiss class from the mini-lesson using practiced signals and behavior.

- Students will write independently at the end of each day's mini-lesson.

Teacher's Note

Focus only on one or two teaching points. Keep in mind that the writing belongs to the student, and you are making suggestions for improvement. Always allow the student to make the changes on his or her own paper.

Teacher's Note

You may want to decide if you want your students to rewrite their story in their best handwriting or if you want them to type it on the computer. If you have an assistant or a parent who can help with the word processing, that may be a way to expedite the publishing. Remember that published writing should be free of errors so that it can be read by others.

DAY 28 – Publishing

Purpose

• Explain the publishing step of the writing process.

Teaching Points

• Call students to the whole-group meeting area using your practiced signal.

• Point out the publishing step in the writing process by referencing the writing process cycle.

• **Say:** *After authors have edited their writing, then they look at the next step in the writing process. This is the publishing step. As authors, we will decide on illustrations that need to be added to the story. In the publishing stage, we reread our writing to make sure the message says what we want it to say. We add any illustrations that are needed.*

• Display the story that was written together on Days 17–19 and reread it with students. Refer to the Writing Process Cycle chart.

• **Say:** *Now we are ready to publish our story. We can do this in many different ways. We are going to create an anchor chart to help us remember the many ways, and we may add to this chart when we think of more ways.*

• Show the students one or two examples of how a piece of writing can be published. Perhaps a bound book (if your school has a binding machine) or one joined with yarn or staples with a construction paper front and back. The cover should include the title, author (author's bio can be placed at the beginning or end of the writing if desired), and an illustration that tells about the story or picture.

• **Say:** *When you are ready, you can decide how your writing will be published and how it will be illustrated.*

• Dismiss class from the mini-lesson using practiced signals and behavior.

• Students will write independently at the end of each day's mini-lesson.

Ways to Publish

1. Make a book.

2. Make a poster.

3. Make a folder book.

etc.

DAY 29 – Publishing, continued

Purpose

- Explain the publishing step of the writing process.
- Discuss text features that could be added to the writing during publication.

Teaching Points

- Call students to the whole-group meeting area using your practiced signal.

- Point out the publishing step in the writing process by referencing the writing process cycle.

- **Say:** *In the publishing stage, we reread our writing to make sure the message says what we want it to say. Then we add any illustrations, charts, or diagrams that are needed. We think about the cover and other features, such as a title page.*

- Display one or more books and point out the importance of a eye-catching cover. Show students the title page and explain why most books contain this page. Then read or thumb through the book to observe the value of the illustrations that are in the book.

- **Say:** *Let's look at the story that we wrote together. What should be on the cover? What would be on the title page? What illustrations would this book need?*

- **Say:** *When you are ready to publish, decide what features you will include in your book.*

- Dismiss class from the mini-lesson using practiced signals and behavior.

- Students will write independently at the end of each day's mini-lesson.

Teacher's Note

You may want to be prepared by having the class book typed so students will be able to see an example of the book in its publishing state. After typing the text and leaving a space for illustrations at the top or bottom of the pages, we usually passed the pages out to partners and let the class illustrate our class book. We then bound the book and placed it centrally in the classroom so students had access and could read the book.

Teacher's Note

You may want to do this lesson now so that students will know what to expect, or you may want to wait until a student is almost ready to share. It is helpful to have one of your own stories that you have published.

DAY 30 – Sharing

Purpose

• Explain the sharing step of the writing process.
• Learn appropriate responses.
• Understand the importance of the author's chair.

Teaching Points

• Call students to the whole-group meeting area using your practiced signal.

• Point out the sharing step in the writing process by referencing the writing process cycle.

• **Say:** *After authors have their writing published, they often like to share their writing with others. This is the sharing step. Authors are proud of what they have written.*

• Display the story that you have written.

• **Say:** *Now I am ready to share our class story. I will sit in the author's chair, and I expect that you will listen carefully to our story. After I read it, I will ask if anyone has questions or comments about my story. You must be a good listener in order to respond appropriately. Let's think of questions or comments that would be appropriate.*

• Make a two-column chart. One column will be "Good Questions" and the other will be "Appropriate Comments." Brainstorm a list of questions and comments, and post it close to the author's chair. Remind students that they can add more to this anchor chart as they think of other questions and comments.

• While sitting in the author's chair, read the class story to the students. Guide them to respond appropriately.

• **Say:** *When you are ready to share your writing, the author's chair will be ready for you.*

• Dismiss class from the mini-lesson using practiced signals and behavior.

• Students will write independently at the end of each day's mini-lesson.

Mini-Lessons:
The First 30 Days of Writer's Workshop in Grades 1 and 2

30 Days of Instruction

DAY 1 – Getting Ready for Writer's Workshop
Whole-Group Instruction and Oral Language Development

Purpose

• Encourage smooth transitions when coming and going to whole-group instruction.
• Show students where and how to sit during whole-group instruction.
• Begin oral language development by reading literature and modeling making connections and storytelling. (Teacher will need some objects reflecting a memory to use during the lesson—such as photos, mementos, etc.)

Teaching Points

• Show students the area where whole-group instruction will occur, and model how you want students to sit when they come to that area. You may want to assign students a place on the carpet so there won't be competition to sit in a certain place.

• Explain and model your signal (i.e. bell, clap, click, calling table groups, etc.) for transitioning students to whole-group instruction.

• Model the procedure for moving to the whole-group area. Then give students the opportunity to practice the procedure and how to sit quietly and attentively.

• **Say:** *When we move to the whole-group area, it will be a time to learn about writing.*

• **Say:** *We will begin Writer's Workshop the same way every day.*

• **Say:** *I have a special book that I want to share with you. The title is **Something from Nothing** by Phoebe Gilman (or any other book that deals with recording thoughts on paper).*

• Read the book to the students stopping a couple of times to think aloud and to model making connections.

• **Say:** *This book made me think about all of the stories in my head, even though I have nothing in my hand. For example, I think about the time (teacher will tell a story of their childhood). Here is a photo of me . . . Here is a memento from the trip . . .*

• Acknowledge any hands that may go up and reinforce the fact that they have made connections.

• **Say:** *Does this make you think of anything that happened to you? Would someone like to share a story they remember?*

• Allow students to tell stories. If any of their stories remind the teacher of a different memory, model the idea of being able to use what others say as a reminder of another story. Continue until the end of the workshop time.

- **Say:** *Many of you told wonderful stories today. Was it fun to hear your memories? Did you enjoy hearing my memories? Remember, we all have memories and stories to tell.*

- Review and model your signal (i.e. bell, clap, click, walking fingers, calling table groups, workstation groups, etc.) for leaving whole-group instruction.

- Use the signal and invite students to go back to their seats.

DAY 2 – Getting Ready for Writer's Workshop
Good Listening Habits and Oral Language Development

Purpose

• Develop good listening habits.
• Introduce and Practice "Turn and Talk."
• Continue with oral language development.

Teaching Points

• Review and practice coming to the whole-group meeting area.

• **Say:** *There will be times when you all will want to share your thoughts. Today we are going to learn a way to do that called "Turn and Talk." When I invite you to turn and talk, you will sit knee to knee and look at your partner to take turns sharing an idea.*

• Teachers may want to assign students a partner they are sitting beside and can work with so the same partner is available each time.

• Choose a student to be your partner and model what it looks like to turn and talk.

• Invite the students to practice turning and talking. Invite them to talk about why it's important to listen to you partner. Make sure they understand they should be knee to knee and looking at their partner.

• After asking students to again focus on the teacher, discuss why it's important to have good listening habits including appropriate noise levels.

• **Say:** *Today I have another special book to share with you. The title is **Wolf!** by Becky Bloom (or any other book that models storytelling).*

• The teacher models making connections with this book and telling another memory.

• **Say:** *I see that many of you have stories you would like to share. Since I know that all of you would like a turn, let's practice our new strategy. Turn and talk to your partner.*

• The teacher will want to listen to the students tell their stories to each other. Pay special attention to good stories that some of the reluctant students have told.

• **Say:** *While listening to the partners, I heard (name) tell a very good story. (Name), will you share your story with the class?*

• Dismiss class practicing signals and behavior when returning to seats or moving on to write independently.

DAY 3 – Getting Ready for Writer's Workshop
Good Listening Habits and Oral Language Development

Purpose

- Develop good listening habits.
- Practice "Turn and Talk."
- Continue with oral language development.

Teaching Points

- Review and practice coming to the whole-group meeting area.

- **Say:** *There will be many times during Writer's Workshop when you listen to a speaker. You may be asked to listen to your teacher when they are talking with you. You may be asked to listen to a friend and you may want your friend to listen to you. When you listen to a speaker, what are some of the important things to remember?*

- Brainstorm and create an anchor chart listing characteristics of a good listener using modeled writing. Title the chart Characteristics of a Good Listener.

- **Say:** *Today I'd like to share a story titled* **Martha Speaks** *by Susan Meddaugh (or another story about animals). Remember to be a good listener as I read the story to you.*

- Read the story to the students and model telling a story you have about animals.

- Remind students of the procedures of turning and talking to a partner.

- **Say:** *I see that many of you have animal stories you would like to share. Since I know that all of you would like a turn, let's practice turning and talking to your partner.*

- The teacher will want to listen to the students tell their stories to each other. Pay special attention to good stories that some of the reluctant students have told.

- **Say:** *While listening to the partners, I heard (name) tell a very good story. (Name), will you share your story with the class?*

- **Ask:** *As we were working on our anchor chart, what did you do today that made you a good listener? What could you do tomorrow to make yourself a better listener? Is there anything you would like to add to our chart?*

- Dismiss class practicing signals and behavior when returning to seats or moving on to write independently.

Characteristics of a Good Listener

1. Look at the speaker.

2. Keep hands to yourself.

3. Sit quietly.

DAY 4 – Getting Ready for Writer's Workshop
Creating a Topic List of Writing Ideas and Oral Language Development

Purpose

- Practice good listening habits.
- Create a list of possible writing topics.
- Continue with oral language development.

Teaching Points

- Review and practice coming to the whole-group meeting area.

- **Say:** *Today I'd like to share another story. This story is titled* **Wilfrid Gordon McDonald Partridge** *by Mem Fox (or* **All the Places to Love** *by Patricia MacLachlan). Remember to be a good listener as I read the story to you.*

- Read the story to the students and model telling a story you have about any connection you can make to the book.

- Remind students of the procedures of turning and talking to a partner.

- **Say:** *I see that many of you have many stories you would like to share. Since I know that all of you would like a turn, let's practice turning and talking to your partner.*

- Listen to the students tell their stories to one another. Pay special attention to good stories that some of the reluctant students have told.

- **Say:** *While I was listening to (name's) story, it reminded me of another story that I have.*

- Tell the story to the students and then **say:** *I have told so many stories and I want to make a list of them. I think I should just write down a few words to help me remember the topic of my stories. For example, I just told you a story about (my grandmother's quilt). I think I should just write down "grandmother's quilt" on my list.*

- Model writing *I can write about . . .* at the top of a piece of chart paper. You will want to have a place to display this list when it is finished. Write a #1 and put "grandmother's quilt" after the number.

- **Say:** *Help me remember what some of my stories were about.*

- As students brainstorm the stories that you told, list them on your chart.

- **Say:** *I loved telling these stories, but I would like to tell the whole story in writing. You may want to write about some of your stories, too!*

- Dismiss class practicing signals and behavior when returning to seats or moving on to write independently.

I can write about . . .

1 grandmother's quilt

DAY 5 – Getting Ready for Writer's Workshop
Creating a Topic List of Writing Ideas and Oral Language Development

Purpose

- Practice good listening habits.
- Create a list of possible writing topics.
- Continue with oral language development.

Teaching Points

- Review and practice coming to the whole-group meeting area.

- **Say:** *Today I'd like to share another story. This story is titled* **Arthur Writes a Story** *by Marc Brown (or another story that centers around writing). Remember to be a good listener as I read the story to you.*

- Read the story to the students and model telling a story you have about any connection you can make to the book.

- **Say:** *I see that many of you have many stories you would like to share. Since I know that all of you would like a turn, let's practice turning and talking to your partner.*

- The teacher will want to listen to the students tell their stories to one another and allow one or two students to share their stories with the whole group.

- **Say:** *All of you have shared many stories with your partner or with the class. Yesterday I made a list of the stories that I have told, and I would like you to be able to list your stories, too. Remember that you have told stories about memories, your family, animals, etc.* (Recap subjects that you have discussed.)

- Display the *I can write about . . .* list that you wrote during Day 4 and remind students how they helped you compile your list.

- **Say:** *Now think about all of the stories that you have told during this week. We will now have time for you to compile a list of all of the stories that you can tell.*

- Distribute paper and ask students to return to their seats to compose their lists. Support students who are struggling to remember some of the stories that they have told.

- After 10–15 minutes, use your signal to call students back to the whole-group meeting area. Ask them to bring their lists with them.

- **Say:** *You have each worked very hard and have listed many of the stories that you have told. Some of you may not have finished your list, but you will have time tomorrow to add to it. Remember that this list will never be finished. You can always add to it whenever you remember a good story or have something that you would like to tell or to write.*

- Dismiss students using your signal.

Teacher's Note

For today's lesson only, the writing time is included in this lesson so that students will be prepared for Day 7.

DAY 6 – Writer's Workshop
Procedures: Using and Storing Writing Folders

Purpose

• Guide students in the proper use and care of their writing folders.
• Help students understand where their folders are stored and how to return them to the storage place.

Teaching Points

• Use your signal to call students to the whole-group meeting area.

• Hold up a folder that you have predetermined each student will use as their writing folder. (Usually these folders are uniform in appearance. They are the same color and type for easy identification as a writing folder.)

• **Say:** *You will each have a folder that looks like this. This is your writing folder. You will want to put your name on your folder. You will use your folder to store all of your writing and other resources writers use. Your topic list will go inside this folder. When we come back for our mini-lesson, you will want to bring your folder with you. We will store our folders* (in a predetermined place) *and return them when Writer's Workshop is over.*

• Model a folder you have assembled with your own writing. Show that your name is on the front of your folder and that you have included pieces of your writing that are "in progress" or "completed." You may want to show that you have stapled your topic sheet on the inside cover.

• **Say:** *Your writing folder is your tool to help you organize your writing and keep your writing from getting lost. It will be one of your most important resources when you write. You will want to keep it with you during Writer's Workshop.*

• **Say:** *We keep our writing folders in the same place each day. It is very important to get and return our folders carefully. We keep them neat and don't bend or tear them. We take care of them since we use them every day.* (Model the storage place and how the folders should look before and after the students have returned their folders to the proper place.)

• **Say:** *Let's practice how to get and replace our folders in a neat, orderly manner.*

• Give each student their writing folder and allow them to practice putting the folder in the storage place.

• Model for the students how to follow the procedure (calling rows, tables, students, etc.) when you are ready to end Writer's Workshop. Practice until the students are able to retrieve and store folders correctly and quietly.

• **Writing Time:** Distribute the topic list that they compiled on Day 5. Ask students to return to their seats. Invite them to place their name on the front of the folder and then add to their topic lists. Suggest that students who are ready might want to begin writing, and they may do so at this time. As students are working, circulate and help students staple their topic lists to their folders.

DAY 7 – Writer's Workshop
Choosing the Writing Topic

Purpose

• Guide students in the process of choosing a topic for writing from their list.

Teaching Points

• Use your signal to call students to the whole-group meeting area.

• The teacher should have his or her own topic list that was compiled with the students available to use for this mini-lesson.

• The students need to have their writing folder with them.

• **Say:** *These are all stories that I could tell and write. This one is one of my favorite stories. I will put a star beside this topic to remind me that I want to write about this first. Now look at your topic list. Decide on your favorite topic. Now turn to your partner and tell the whole story.*

• **Say:** *When you hear the signal, please take your writing folder and go back to your seat to write or draw what you told your partner.*

• Distribute paper to the students.

• Dismiss students from the mini-lesson using your signal.

My Topic List

1. Memories

2. My best friend

3. My family

4. My new pet

DAY 8 – Concept of Writer's Workshop

Purpose

- Introduce concept of Writer's Workshop to students.
- Clarify the purpose of Writer's Workshop.

Teaching Points

- Use your signal to call students to the whole-group meeting area.

- **Say:** *Today we will be talking about Writer's Workshop and what it is.*

- Draw a blank three-column chart. As you explain and discuss the components (mini-lesson, independent writing time, and sharing time) of Writer's Workshop, you will complete the chart.

- Begin by explaining the mini-lesson. Write "Mini-Lesson" at the top of the first column.

- **Say:** *We have been learning about how we come together as a whole group to learn more about writing. This is one part of Writer's Workshop.*

- Write a few ideas in the Mini-Lesson column.

- Write "Writing Time" at the top of the second column. Explain that students will be doing different things during writing time. Explain that most of their writing time will be spent writing and using the writing process. Explain that the students will be learning about the writing process during their mini-lessons.

- **Say:** *After our mini-lesson, we will use what we learn about writing to write stories or pieces of writing that interest us. We will use the writing process when we write, so each of us may be at different places in the writing process.*

- Write a few ideas in the Writing Time column.

- Write "Sharing Time" at the top of the third column. Explain the students will have an opportunity to share what they have written with other students in the class. Explain that they will also hear what others have written.

- **Say:** *There will be times to share with the group or a partner about things you have written. You may get help from your friends about a writing problem, read an especially interesting part of your writing to a friend, or listen to a friend's writing as they read to you.*

- Write a few ideas in the Sharing Time column.

- Ask students to share ideas about how Writer's Workshop will help them become better writers.

- Dismiss students from the mini-lesson using your signal.

- Students will write independently at the end of each day's mini-lesson.

Writer's Workshop

Mini-Lesson	Writing Time	Sharing Time
1. Learn about writing	1. Draft	1. Good listening
2. Whole Group	2. Edit	2. Share each other's writing
3. Story	3. Conference	3. Ask questions
4. Writing	4. Revise	
	5. Think about a story	

DAY 9 – Writer's Workshop Procedures
Using and Storing Writing Tools

Purpose

- Introduce students to storage places for writing tools.
- Guide students in the proper use and storage of materials.

Teaching Points

- Use your signal to call students to the whole-group meeting area.

- Tell your students that today you are going to tell them about a place in your room where they will find many things they will need as writers. Invite your class to come with you to the writing table or to the location in the classroom where materials will be stored. Tell your students that these are resources that they will need when writing books. (Have several different tools there to share with the students. Suggestions: loose leaf notebook paper, unlined paper, construction paper, stapler, tape, hole punch, rulers, scissors, pens for editing, sharpened pencils, markers, dictionaries, thesauri, etc.) Take the time to talk about each item, emphasizing that these are tools, not toys. Help students understand that it will be their responsibility to use them wisely and for the correct purpose.

- **Say:** *As we learn about the writing process during our mini-lessons, you will see how we use these tools.*

- Invite the students to return to the whole-group meeting area and find their seat. Debrief the location of the writing tools and their use. Create an anchor chart titled "Tools Students Use When Writing." Invite the students to help list the tools and note how each tool is used. Post the anchor chart over the writing table or in the writing area.

- Dismiss students from the mini-lesson using your signal.

- Students will write independently at the end of each day's mini-lesson.

Tools Students Use When Writing

1. notebook paper
2. unlined paper
3. pencils/pens
4. stapler

Looks Like	Sounds Like

DAY 10 – Writer's Workshop Procedures
Creating an Effective Atmosphere for Writers

Purpose

- Guide students in developing rules for Writer's Workshop.
- Help students understand what Writer's Workshop looks like and sounds like.

Teaching Points

- Call students to the whole-group meeting area using your practiced signal.

- Using the anchor charts, review with students what makes a good listener and what Writer's Workshop is.

- **Say:** *We know that during Writer's Workshop we learn about writing. There are ways that we can work together to make our classroom a better place to write. Today we are going to brainstorm what we can do to make our classroom a place where we can work and write together.*

- Introduce a two-column T-Chart that will help students clarify what Writer's Workshop looks like and sounds like. Title the two columns "Looks Like" and "Sounds Like." This is a fluid chart that you will add to during the year as your Workshop develops.

- **Say:** *Use only your eyes. What would you see if you walked into our room during Writer's Workshop?* (i.e. students sitting on the floor in whole group for the mini-lesson, students talking with the teacher, students talking and writing with one another, students writing independently, students sharing, etc.)

- Record students' ideas on the T-Chart under the column "Looks Like."

- **Say:** *Use only your ears. What would you hear if you walked into our room during Writer's Workshop?* (i.e. students using tools, pencils scratching, students moving around the room quietly, students quietly sharing with partners and/or a teacher, the teacher teaching a mini-lesson, etc.)

- Record students' ideas on the T-Chart under the column "Sounds Like."

- Use the anchor charts as resources to revisit when you face problematic situations during your Workshop.

- Dismiss students from the mini-lesson using your signal.

- Students will write independently at the end of each day's mini-lesson.

DAY 11 – Writer's Workshop Procedures
Appropriate Behavior

Purpose

• Discuss behavior that is appropriate and conducive to writing.

Teaching Points

• Use your signal to call students to the whole-group meeting area.

• **Say:** *When I am writing, I need to be able to think about my good ideas and put those ideas in writing. I can't write well if someone is bothering me. What helps you to do your best thinking and writing? What helps Writer's Workshop run smoothly?*

• Brainstorm a list of appropriate behaviors and post them on a chart entitled "Writer's Workshop Rules." These rules could include:
  —You may participate in the writing process during the entire time.
  —You may not disturb others.
  —You may sit in a comfortable place.
  —Listen when asked.
  —Be ready to share when asked.
  —Make sure you get and replace your writing folder at the proper time, etc.

• **Say:** *I will place our rules on the wall so that we can refer to them at any time. In addition, if we think of other rules that we need to add, we can do that.*

• **Say:** *Be sure that you follow our workshop rules as you write today and every day.*

• Dismiss students using your signal.

Writer's Workshop Rules

• You may not disturb others.

• You may sit in a comfortable place.

• Listen when asked.

• Be ready to share when asked.

DAY 12 – Writer's Workshop Procedures
Where to Sit

Purpose

• Guide students in sitting in the location that is most conducive to writing.
• Help students understand where and when they might move to a new location to write.

Teaching Points

• Use your signal to call students to the whole-group meeting area.

• Model sitting at your desk to write something.

• **Say:** *Is this the only place in the classroom that you have seen me write? What other places have you noticed me writing?*

• Brainstorm a list of places that students have seen you engaged in writing.

• **Say:** *You have noticed that there are many places in this classroom that I can write, and there are reasons why I might need to move to another location. As writers, you might be very comfortable writing at your desk, but there may be other places in this classroom that you might also be able to write. Let's create a chart to help us remember good places to write.*

• Create a web on chart paper that students can use as an anchor chart. Note any appropriate places that children might be able to sit during writing time (a table in the classroom, a corner that is away from others, a desk beside another student while conferring, on the floor, etc.).

• **Say:** *You can move to any place in the classroom that is comfortable and helps you to stay focused while you are writing. Remember that this must be a place where you are not disturbing others while they are writing.*

• **Say:** *Now let's practice finding a good place to write as we continue with Writer's Workshop.*

• Dismiss students using your signal.

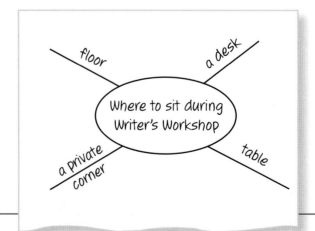

DAY 13 – Introduce the Writing Process

Purpose

- Review the prewriting piece of Writer's Workshop.
- Create an anchor chart with the writing process cycle.

Teaching Points

- Call students to the whole-group meeting area using your practiced signal.

- **Say:** *Today we're going to begin learning about the process good writers use when they are writing a story or any piece of writing. Most authors follow this cycle or one very similar to it every time they create a piece of writing. Since we're authors too, we want to learn how this cycle, or writing process, will help us be better writers. We have been writing stories and placing them in our writing folders. Now we will learn what we can do next.*

- Show students the list of stories that you made on Day 5. Add another topic to your list that concerns something that happened at school. The story should be one that students can contribute thoughts and ideas. Tell them that tomorrow they will help you write that story.

- **Say:** *Be thinking about ideas for the story that we will write tomorrow.*

- Dismiss class from the mini-lesson using practiced signals and behavior.

- Students will write independently at the end of each day's mini-lesson.

Teacher's Note

It will be important to post a visual that will help students reflect on the writing process. The visual should be in a spot in the room that is accessible and continuously available for reference. (See figure below for a suggested format.)

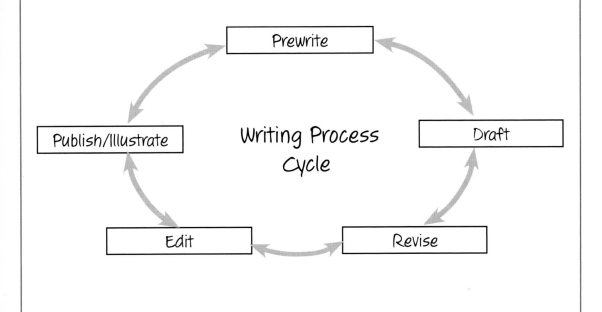

Teacher's Note

This is an excellent opportunity to begin creating a risk-free atmosphere in your room by accepting all ideas and allowing students to decide the direction of the story. Remember: This is a short story that will be used to model the writing process. Too many details will create a story that will be lengthy and hard to use for modeling purposes.

DAY 14 – Continue Prewriting Using a Web

Purpose

• Explain to students the importance of prewriting.
• Create a story web.

Teaching Points

• Call students to the whole-group meeting area using your practiced signal.

• Revisit the brainstorming process and remind students about the new idea that they will all help to write.

• **Say:** *When good writers begin a story or any writing, they use a tool to help them record their ideas so they can think about their story in an organized way. One of the tools some writers choose to use is a web. Today, we're going to use the idea we decided on yesterday to create a web for our story.*

• On a piece of chart paper, draw a circle in the center with the idea students chose to write about written in the center of the circle. Around that idea, write or draw the details as students brainstorm creating a web that will drive the direction of the story or event. Be sure to guide students into including the literary elements of character, setting, problem, and solution. (See example below.)

• Dismiss class from the mini-lesson using practiced signals and behavior.

• Students will write independently at the end of each day's mini-lesson.

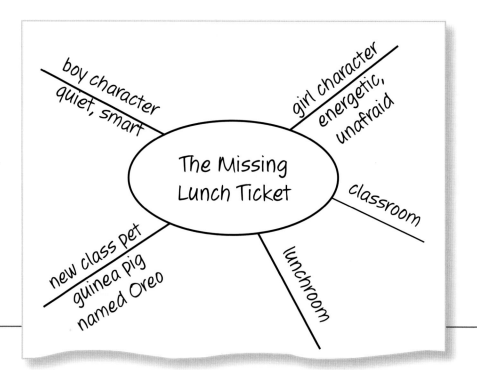

DAY 15 – Continue Prewriting

Purpose

• Create an anchor chart showing different kinds of prewriting.

Teaching Points

• Call students to the whole-group meeting area using your practiced signal.

• **Say:** *We have been using a web to do our prewriting for our story. As you practice writing, you may choose other ways to prewrite. Today we are going to create an anchor chart with different ideas about prewriting. The chart may help you choose a way to prewrite that will help you organize ideas for a piece of writing.*

• Using a piece of chart paper, title the anchor chart "Prewriting." Invite your students to give ideas of different ways to prewrite. (make lists, draw pictures, brainstorm, use graphic organizers, etc.)

• **Say:** *After you have finished your prewriting, remember to store that paper in your writing folders so you have it when you begin writing your story.*

• Dismiss class from the mini-lesson using practiced signals and behavior.

• Students will write independently at the end of each day's mini-lesson.

Prewriting

1. Make lists

2. Draw pictures

3. Brainstorm

4. Graphic organizer

DAY 16 – Continue Prewriting

Purpose

- Review the prewriting step of the writing.
- Know that each story has a beginning, middle, and end.
- Create an anchor chart showing the characteristics of a beginning, middle, and end of a story.

Teaching Points

- Make sure you have the writing process anchor chart posted in a place where you can easily refer to the writing process cycle. Call attention to the writing process cycle and review the process of prewriting. Talk with your class about the next step in the process—rough draft.

- **Say:** *When a writer is ready to begin writing the rough draft, it is important to look over the prewriting and think about where to start writing. Every story has a beginning. In the beginning, an author may put the character and setting.*

- Use the class prewriting from Day 13 and identify the character and setting.

- **Say:** *Every story has a middle. In the middle, a writer tells what in happening in the story. This may sound like a problem in the story.*

- Use the class prewriting to identify the points that may be in the middle of the story.

- **Say:** *Every story has an ending. In the end, a writer could tell how a problem is solved.*

- Use the class prewriting to identify the points that could be in the ending of the story.

- **Say:** *When we start writing our story, it will be important to use our prewriting to help us make sure we don't leave any part of our story out.*

- Using chart paper, create a three-column T-Chart. Title the first column "Beginning," the second column "Middle," and the third column "End." Invite the class to contribute ideas of what a writer could put in the beginning of a story (details describing a character[s], details describing the setting, etc.), in the middle of a story (details describing a problem, events leading up to a problem, how a character reacts to the problem, etc.), and at the end of a story (details describing how a problem is solved, how a character feels about the solutions, how the solution affects the character, etc.).

- Post the anchor chart where students can use it for a reference to write the rough draft of the story.

- Dismiss class from the mini-lesson using practiced signals and behavior.

- Students will write independently at the end of each day's mini-lesson.

Beginning	Middle	End
Character Setting Event	Problem Events	Solution Feelings of characters

Day 17 – Begin Rough Draft Step of Writing Process Cycle

Purpose

- Review the Beginning, Middle, and End Anchor Chart.
- Understand that the rough draft is written on every other line.
- Begin writing the rough draft of your class story.

Teaching Points

- Call students to the whole-group meeting area using your practiced signal.

- It is important to have the writing process posted in a place where you can easily refer to the writing process cycle. Call attention to the writing process cycle and review the process of prewriting. Talk with the class about the next step in the process—rough draft.

- **Say:** *When a writer is ready to start writing a rough draft, the first thing that an author does is look at the prewriting to see where he or she wants to start. The last time we met, we identified the points that we could put at the beginning of our rough draft.*

- **Say:** *When an author is writing the rough draft, it is important that his or her attention is on putting thoughts on paper. You will probably make some spelling errors, grammar errors, or have story elements you will eventually want to change. The most important thing about a rough draft is that you spend your time writing and putting your ideas on paper.*

- **Say:** *It is also important to remember that we will write on every other line. Writers do this because there will come a time when they will need that extra line to fix up the story.*

- Using a piece of chart paper, begin the process of writing the rough draft of your class story. (Be sure that you skip lines on the paper.) Invite the class to contribute ideas for the story using the prewriting web and chart as a guide.

- Begin writing the rough draft, inviting students to contribute sentences and ideas for the beginning of the class story. Continue with this process until your mini-lesson time is up. Tell the students that you will continue with the story tomorrow. You will use your mini-lesson time for the next couple of days until the rough draft for your story is complete.

- Dismiss class from the mini-lesson using practiced signals and behavior.

- Students will write independently at the end of each day's mini-lesson.

Teacher's Note

It's important to emphasize that, even though the rough draft is not the time to use a dictionary to look up words or ask how to spell words correctly, there are many words that the students do know how to spell. Your expectation is that these words are not to be misspelled. Students will be at different developmental writing and spelling stages. A word wall is an important tool for students to reference at this time.

Teacher's Note

You will want to encourage your students to reread often. They need to make sure that their writing makes sense and that their message conveys what they intended.

DAYS 18–19 – Continue Writing Process Cycle
Rough Draft

Purpose

• Continue using the writing process cycle (rough draft) to create a class story emphasizing a beginning, middle, and end to the story.

Teaching Points

• Call students to the whole-group meeting area using your practiced signal.

• **Say:** *Today we will continue writing the rough draft of our story. Who knows what part of our story we are ready to draft? How do you know?* (By looking at our prewriting and looking at the points we want to write about.)

• Reread the rough draft of what has been written so far. Continue writing the rough draft until your mini-lesson time is over.

• You will use your mini-lesson time for a couple of days to complete the rough draft.

• Dismiss class from the mini-lesson using practiced signals and behavior.

• Students will write independently at the end of each day's mini-lesson.

DAY 20 – Completing the Rough Draft

Purpose

• Create an anchor chart entitled "Rough Draft."

Teaching Points

• Call students to the whole-group meeting area using your practiced signal.

• **Say:** *We have been writing the rough draft of our story. Let's create an anchor chart about the important points of a rough draft.*

• Using a piece of chart paper, title the anchor chart "Rough Draft." Invite the students to contribute ideas about writing a rough draft. (Write many sentences; follow your prewriting plan; write all of your story; make sure you write a beginning, middle, and end in your story; make sure you have characters, setting, problem and solution; correctly spell words that you know; put down what you know about words that you don't know, etc.)

• Post the rough draft anchor chart beside the prewriting anchor chart. This assures availability to the students when working their way through the writing process cycle.

• Dismiss class from the mini-lesson using practiced signals and behavior.

• Students will write independently at the end of each day's mini-lesson.

Rough Draft

1. Write many sentences.

2. Follow prewrite.

3. Write all of the story.

4. Write a beginning, middle, and end.

DAY 21 – Introduce Revising
Using a Caret

Purpose

• Introduce students to the revising step of the writing process cycle.
• Use completed class story to model revising concept.
• Model the use of a caret as a revision tool used to insert one or two words.

Teaching Points

• Call students to the whole-group meeting area using your practiced signal.

• **Say:** *Do you remember what a good reader does after they finish reading? That's right. They go back and think about their reading. A good writer does about the same thing. After an author has written the rough draft, a good writer goes back over their writing and thinks about how their story sounds. There are many things to think about. An author may think about the character, setting, problem, and solution. They may think about using describing words, adding sentences to make their writing clearer, or adding whole chunks to a story to make it more exciting or easier for their audience to read. Today we're going to look at one way to revise your writing.*

• Reread the story that the class wrote together. While you read, think aloud to model the process of adding adjectives to provide description.

• **Say:** *I'm reading this sentence. It says that . . .* (For example: "It says that the bear was chasing the rabbit into the forest. I ask myself what kind of bear it was. Was it a baby bear? Was it a big bear? Was it fat? Was it hungry?") *I think that we could add words to this sentence to make it more interesting. We could also help the reader visualize the . . . What words do you think we could add to this sentence?*

• Continue through the story finding appropriate places to use the caret. Then write an adjective above the caret on the blank line that is formed as lines are skipped during writing. Use some discretion when choosing words so that there are only a few examples.

• **Say:** *When you are ready to make revisions to your story, you may want to try using a caret if you just need to add one or two words.*

• Dismiss class from the mini-lesson using practiced signals and behavior.

• Students will write independently at the end of each day's mini-lesson.

The Missing Lunch Ticket

"But I had my $\wedge$ lunch

ticket right here!"

Jose looked $\wedge$ everywhere for it

again. The ticket

has disappeared.

DAY 22 – Continue Revising
Using Spider Legs

Purpose

- Model the use of a spider leg as a revision tool used when adding one or two sentences to a rough draft.

Teaching Points

- Call students to the whole-group meeting area using your practiced signal.

- **Say:** *The step of the writing process that we've been learning about is revising. This step is difficult for some writers because it's hard to change what they have written. Remember that, when we make revisions, we are making our writing more interesting, more accurate, and more complete. There are times when we revise that we may need to add more than a word to our writing. We many want to add a sentence. We're going to use a tool called a spider leg.*

- Read through the class story to find a place where another sentence could be added for clarity or detail.

- Model cutting a strip of writing paper and taping it on the draft where you want to add the sentence.

- **Say:** *Now you're ready to write your sentence(s) on this strip of paper. When you read the story, read this sentence with the rest of your story.*

- Continue modeling using the spider leg revision tool by inviting the class to find one or two different places where a sentence could be added to the rough draft that was written in class on Days 17–19.

- **Say:** *When you are ready to make revisions to your story, you may want to try using this tool. The strips are already cut. You can find them back on the writing table (or any place that would be convenient for students).*

- Dismiss class from the mini-lesson using practiced signals and behavior.

- Students will write independently at the end of each day's mini-lesson.

The Missing Lunch Ticket

"But I had my ^lunch ticket right here!"

next to the guinea pig's cage

José looked ^everywhere for it again. The ticket has disappeared.

José was so sad.

DAY 23 – Continue Revising
Using an Asterisk

Purpose

• Model the use of an asterisk as a revision tool to add a paragraph to a rough draft.

Teaching Points

• Call students to the whole-group meeting area using your practiced signal.

• **Say:** *Sometimes when we revise our writing, we decide that we want to add a paragraph to our writing in order to make our writing more interesting or to help answer questions our audience may have about our writing. When we want to add several sentences to our writing, we use a revision tool called an asterisk. It looks like this: *.*

• Refer to the class story. Reread the class story reading adjectives added by using a caret and sentences added by using a spider leg. After rereading, invite the class to contribute ideas about places where a paragraph or several sentences could be added to increase the readers' interest in the story.

• Decide with the class where the sentences need to be placed and what the sentences should say. Then, place an *1 where you want to make the revision. On separate sheet of chart paper, also place an *1 and write the paragraph. If there is another paragraph added, place an *2 where you want to make the revision. On the separate sheet of paper, add *2 and write the paragraph. Reread the story after every revision to make sure it sounds correct.

• **Say:** *If you need to add many sentences to your writing when you make revisions, you may want to try using an asterisk.*

• Dismiss class from the mini-lesson using practiced signals and behavior.

• Students will write independently at the end of each day's mini-lesson.

* All of the students came to help José. Some students looked under chairs, others . . .

DAY 24 – Introduce Response Groups

Purpose

- Explain what a response group is.
- Model what a response group looks like and sounds like.
- Create an anchor chart about revision tools and how they're used.

Teaching Points

- Call students to the whole-group meeting area using your practiced signal.

- **Say:** *We have learned several ways to revise our writing. Today we will create an anchor chart titled "Revising."*

- Invite the students to give ideas about revising and what methods they could use to revise. (Carets are used when adding one or two words; Spider Legs are used when adding sentences; Asterisks are used when adding paragraphs; Response groups are used to help an author revise, etc.)

- Post the anchor chart with the Prewrite and Rough Draft anchor charts. Remind the students to use these charts as a resource as they move through the writing process cycle.

- **Say:** *When you are ready to begin the revisions on your writing, it helps to have someone listen to your writing and give you ideas. Today we are going to use a response group to help us revise. A response group is a group of three sitting knee to knee and eye to eye. The purpose is to give an author a place to read the story and talk with an audience about the story.*

- Invite a group of three students to sit on the floor in a triangle. They are close enough that a soft voice can be heard and used, but not close enough to touch. Inform the class that the person who asks for a response group is the author of a piece of writing. They then choose two people to join them in the group. Choose one of the group to act as the author. You may want that student to read a piece of their own writing or use the class story.

- Model by having the author read the story and by having the other two students respond to the reading. Remind the students that respect and kindness are always used when participating in a response group. If students have difficulty with this, you might want to become one of the "students" in the group in order to model an appropriate response.

- **Say:** *You may want to call a response group when you are ready to revise. Only two response groups may be held at one time. This is the place where you may have your response groups.*

- Dismiss class from the mini-lesson using practiced signals and behavior.

- Students will write independently at the end of each day's mini-lesson.

Teacher's Note

If your students are not familiar with the process of listening and responding to another student's writing, it will be necessary to provide guidelines before attempting this. You may want to have a separate mini-lesson to create an anchor chart titled "Response Groups" with suggestions from the following list: Listen politely. Ask questions to help the author develop the story. Use positive comments. Make kind suggestions to help with detail or answer questions you may have.

Revising

1. Use carets for 1 or 2 words.

2. Use spider legs to add sentences.

3. Use asterisks to add paragraphs.

DAY 25 - Introduce Editing

Purpose

• Introduce students to editing.

Teaching Points

• Call students to the whole-group meeting area using your practiced signal.

• Point out the editing step in the writing process by referencing the writing process cycle.

• **Say:** *After authors have revised their writing, then they look at the next step in the writing process. This is the editing step. It is important that writing has no spelling, capitalization, or punctuation errors. The first step is for the author to look for mistakes by rereading. Then an author often asks someone to help them continue the process. You will do the same thing when you ask someone to be your editor. Your editor will help you read through your writing to look for errors. During the year, we will learn many new things about grammar, capitalization, punctuation, and spelling. You will be expected to use what we learn as you edit your own writing and the writing of others.*

• Edit your class story or a story that has at least one spelling error, one capitalization error, and one punctuation error. Invite students to correct errors they see as you read the story.

• **Say:** *You may be ready to edit your writing. Remember to reread your writing to find and correct as many errors as possible before asking a classmate to be your editor.*

• Dismiss class from the mini-lesson using practiced signals and behavior.

• Students will write independently at the end of each day's mini-lesson.

Teacher's Note

Common editing marks are included on page 180. You will be the best judge as to the levels of mastery your students will have when identifying spelling, punctuation, and capitalization errors. You may want to create a chart for your students to use as a resource with the editing marks noted.

DAY 26 – Editing, continued

Purpose

- Explain that conferring with the teacher is part of the editing step of the writing process.
- Make an anchor chart about what to do as they wait to confer with the teacher.

Teaching Points

- Call students to the whole-group meeting area using your practiced signal.

- Point out the editing step in the writing process by referencing the writing process cycle.

- **Say:** *After authors have edited their writing with a partner, they are almost ready to publish their writing.*

- Display the story that was written together on Days 17–19 and reread it with students. Refer to the Writing Process Cycle chart.

- **Say:** *Now that we are almost ready to publish our story, we need to confer with the teacher, who will be your editor-in-chief, the person in charge of publications. This is part of the editing process. I will be your editor-in-chief. When you get the editor-in-chief's approval, you may begin the publishing process.*

- Hold up a spiral or a loose-leaf notebook that is labeled "Conference with Teacher."

- **Say:** *You will sign your name in this notebook when you have revised, edited, and then reread your writing. When you sign, I may be busy working with other students, but this is your way of letting me know that you are almost ready to publish. I will get to you as soon as I can. In the meantime, you have choices about what you can do. You can begin to write something new. Since we know that Writer's Workshop is never finished, what other things could you do while you are waiting for a conference with me?*

- Create a web with "What to Do as I Wait for a Conference" in the center. Students might suggest: finish another piece of writing, edit with another student, be part of a response group, add to the topic list, begin a new draft, etc.

- **Say:** *There may be other times during the writing process that you need to confer with the editor-in-chief. I want you to know that you are welcome to sign the notebook at any time—if you are stuck or if you need help in any way.*

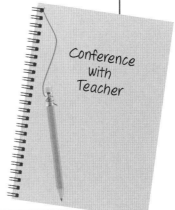

- Refer again to the Writing Process Cycle. Make it clear to students that they must revise, edit, and reread before they are ready to confer.

- Indicate where the notebook will be placed. It's a good idea to use yarn or a string to tie a pencil to the notebook.

- Dismiss class from the mini-lesson using practiced signals and behavior.

- Students will write independently at the end of each day's mini-lesson.

What to Do as I Wait for a Conference

- finish another piece of writing

- edit with another student

- be part of a response group

- add to the topic list

- prewrite

- begin a draft

etc.

DAY 27 – Conferring with the Teacher

Purpose

- Discuss the procedures of teacher/student conferences and their importance.

Teaching Points

- Call students to the whole-group meeting area using your practiced signal.

- Point out the editing step with students and review with them what they need to do during this step of the writing process.

- **Say:** *After authors have edited their writing with their other writers, then they need to talk to the editor-in-chief. We will review your writing once again to ensure that it is ready for publication. We will read your piece together, and then we might focus on one, or possibly two, items that would improve your writing. You might choose to make any changes to your writing during the conference, or you might decide to go back to your writing place to do your final work. You need to have the approval of the editor-in-chief before you begin to publish.*

- **Say:** *Let's review the writing process. If we have revised and edited our writing, we are almost ready to publish. What should we do now? Yes, we sign the conference notebook so that we can meet with the editor-in-chief. When the teacher is ready to confer, we bring our writing folder and our pencil to the conference table. We are prepared to read our writing with the editor-in-chief.*

- Model the conferring process by selecting a student to sit with you and read his or her story. Tell something that you liked about the writing, and be supportive of the student's efforts. Then select one teaching point or suggestion for this student. Ask the student what he or she thinks about your suggestion, and ask if he or she would like to make that change.

- **Say:** *When you have revised, edited, and reread your paper, you are ready to confer with the editor-in-chief. Some of you might be ready for this part of the editing process.*

- Dismiss class from the mini-lesson using practiced signals and behavior.

- Students will write independently at the end of each day's mini-lesson.

Teacher's Note

Focus only on one or two teaching points. Keep in mind that the writing belongs to the student, and you are making suggestions for improvement. Always allow the student to make the changes on his or her own paper.

Teacher's Note

You may want to decide if you want your students to rewrite their story in their best handwriting or if you want them to type it on the computer. If you are fortunate enough to have an assistant or a parent that can help with the word processing, that may be a way to expedite the publishing. Remember that published writing should be free of errors so that it can be read by others.

DAY 28 – Publishing

Purpose

• Explain the publishing step of the writing process.

Teaching Points

• Call students to the whole-group meeting area using your practiced signal.

• Point out the publishing step in the writing process by referencing the writing process cycle.

• **Say:** *After authors have edited their writing, then they look at the next step in the writing process. This is the publishing step. As authors, we will decide on illustrations that need to be added to the story. In the publishing stage, we reread our writing to make sure the message says what we want it to say. We add any illustrations that are needed.*

• Display the story that was written together on Days 17–19 and reread it with students. Refer to the Writing Process Cycle chart.

• **Say:** *Now we are ready to publish our story. We can do this in many different ways. We are going to create an anchor chart to help us remember the many ways, and we may add to this chart when we think of more ways.*

• Brainstorm a list of final products, such as standard books, folder books, accordion books, flip books, shape books, posters, a script, newspaper or magazine articles, blogs, etc. If possible, show students examples of each of these types of publications.

• **Say:** *When you are ready, you can decide how your writing will be published and how it will be illustrated.*

• Dismiss class from the mini-lesson using practiced signals and behavior.

• Students will write independently at the end of each day's mini-lesson.

> Ways to Publish
> 1. Make a book.
> 2. Make a poster.
> 3. Make a folder book.
> etc.

DAY 29 – Publishing, continued

Purpose

- Explain the publishing step of the writing process.
- Discuss text features that could be added to the writing during publication.

Teaching Points

- Call students to the whole-group meeting area using your practiced signal.

- Point out the publishing step in the writing process by referencing the writing process cycle.

- **Say:** *In the publishing stage, we reread our writing to make sure the message says what we want it to say. Then we add any illustrations, charts, or diagrams that are needed. We think about the cover and other features, such as a title page.*

- Display one or more books and point out the importance of a eye-catching cover. Show students the title page and explain why most books contain this page. Then read or thumb through the book to observe the value of the illustrations that are in the book.

- **Say:** *Let's look at the story that we wrote together. What should be on the cover? What would be on the title page? What illustrations would this book need?*

- **Say:** *When you are ready to publish, decide what features you will include in your book.*

- Dismiss class from the mini-lesson using practiced signals and behavior.

- Students will write independently at the end of each day's mini-lesson.

Teacher's Note

You may want to do this lesson now so that students will know what to expect, or you may want to wait until a student is almost ready to share. It is helpful to have one of your own stories that you have published.

DAY 30 – Sharing

Purpose

- Explain the sharing step of the writing process.
- Learn appropriate responses.
- Understand the importance of the author's chair.

Teaching Points

- Call students to the whole-group meeting area using your practiced signal.

- Point out the sharing step in the writing process by referencing the writing process cycle.

- **Say:** *After authors have their writing published, they often like to share their writing with others. This is the sharing step. Authors are proud of what they have written.*

- Display the story that you have written.

- **Say:** *Now I am ready to share our class story. I will sit in the author's chair, and I expect that you will listen carefully to our story. After I read it, I will ask if anyone has questions or comments about my story. You must be a good listener in order to respond appropriately. Let's think of questions or comments that would be appropriate.*

- Make a two-column chart. One column will be "Good Questions" and the other will be "Appropriate Comments." Brainstorm a list of questions and comments, and post it close to the author's chair. Remind students that they can add more to this anchor chart as they think of other questions and comments.

- While sitting in the author's chair, read the class story to the students. Guide them to respond appropriately.

- **Say:** *When you are ready to share your writing, the author's chair will be ready for you.*

- Dismiss class from the mini-lesson using practiced signals and behavior.

- Students will write independently at the end of each day's mini-lesson.

Mini-Lessons:
The First 30 Days of Writer's Workshop in Grades 3–6

30 Days of Instruction

Teacher's Note

The first week of lessons will be for the entire workshop time. There will be no independent write for this week. This week will focus on building oral language and developing the joy of writing.

DAY 1 – Preparing for Writer's Workshop
Whole-Group Instruction and Building Oral Language

Purpose

- Encourage smooth transitions when coming and going to whole-group instruction.
- Show students where and how to sit during whole-group instruction.
- Begin oral language development by reading literature and modeling making connections and storytelling. (Teacher will need some objects reflecting a memory to use during the lesson—such as photos, mementos, etc.)

Teaching Points

- During Writer's Workshop, collaboration and camaraderie are best built when students can come together in a central meeting place. Show students the area where whole-group writing instruction will occur, and model how you expect students to sit when they come to that area. Teachers often assign students a place on the floor or on the carpet so there won't be competition to sit in a certain place.

- Explain and model your signal (i.e. bell, clap, click, calling table groups, etc.) for transitioning students to whole-group instruction for Writer's Workshop.

- Model the procedure for moving to the whole-group area. Then give students the opportunity to practice the procedure and how to sit quietly and attentively.

- **Say:** *When we move to the meeting area, this will be a time to learn more about writing.*

- **Say:** *We will begin Writer's Workshop the same way every day.*

- **Say:** *Today I have a book that I want to share with you. The title is **Something from Nothing** by Phoebe Gilman (or any other book that deals with recording thoughts on paper).*

- Read this picture book to the students, stopping at times to think aloud and to model making text-to-self or text-to-text connections.

- **Say:** *This book made me think about the many stories, or personal narratives, in my head, even though I have nothing in my hand. For example, I think about the time (teacher will tell a personal narrative of his or her childhood). Here is a photo of me . . . Here is a memento from the trip . . .*

- Acknowledge any hands that may go up and reinforce the fact that they have made connections.

- **Say:** *Does this make you think of anything that happened when you were younger? Would some of you like to share a personal narrative about something you remember?*

- Allow students to tell stories. If any of their stories remind the teacher of a different memory, model the idea of being able to use what others say as a reminder of another personal narrative. Continue until the end of the workshop time.

- **Say:** *I really enjoyed hearing some of your memories, and I hope that you have enjoyed hearing mine. Remember, we all have memories and stories to tell.*

- Review and model your signal for leaving whole-group instruction.

- Use the signal and invite students to go back to their seats.

DAY 2 – Preparing for Writer's Workshop
Establishing Routines, Building Oral Language

Purpose

• Build listening skills.
• Introduce and Practice "Turn and Talk."
• Continue with oral language development.

Teaching Points

• Review and practice coming to the whole-group meeting area.

• **Say:** *There will be times when you all will want to share your thoughts. Today we are going to learn a way to do that called "Turn and Talk." When I invite you to turn and talk, you will sit knee to knee and look at your partner to take turns sharing an idea.*

• Teachers may want to assign students a partner they are sitting beside and can work with so the same partner is available each time.

• Choose a student to be your partner and model what it looks like to turn and talk.

• Invite the students to practice turning and talking. Invite them to talk about why it's important to listen to you partner. Make sure they understand they should be knee to knee and looking at and listening to their partner.

• After asking students to again focus on the teacher, discuss why it's important to have good listening habits including appropriate noise levels.

• **Say:** *Although you are great readers, there is much that we can learn from picture books. Today I have another book to share with you. The title is* **Wolf!** *by Becky Bloom (or any other book that models storytelling).*

• The teacher models making connections with this book and telling another memory.

• **Say:** *Many of you have shared memories with the group. Since I know that all of you have memories to tell, let's practice our new strategy. Turn and talk to your partner about one of your memories.*

• The teacher will want to listen to the students tell their stories to each other. Pay special attention to good personal narratives that some of the reluctant students have told.

• **Say:** *While listening to the partners, I heard (name) tell a very personal narrative. (Name), will you share your personal narrative with the class?*

• Dismiss class practicing signals and behavior when returning to seats or moving on to write independently.

DAY 3 – Preparing for Writer's Workshop
Establishing Routines, Building Oral Language

Purpose

- Build listening skills
- Practice "Turn and Talk."
- Continue with oral language development.

Teaching Points

- Review and practice coming to the whole-group meeting area.

- **Say:** *There will be many times during Writer's Workshop when you listen to a speaker. You may be asked to listen to your teacher when they are talking. You may be asked to listen to a classmate and you may want your classmate to listen to you. When you listen to a speaker, what are some of the important things to remember?*

- Brainstorm and create an anchor chart listing characteristics of a good listener using interactive or shared writing. Title the chart Characteristics of a Good Listener.

- **Say:** *Today I'd like to share another narrative titled **Martha Speaks** by Susan Meddaugh (or another narrative about animals). I am expecting that you will be a good listener as I read.*

- Read the book to the students and model telling a personal narrative you have about animals.

- Remind students of the procedures of turning and talking to a partner.

- **Say:** *I see that many of you have narratives about pets or other animals that you have seen. Since I would like for each of you to have an opportunity to share your stories, let's practice turning and talking to your partner. Tell them about one of your pets or an animal you remember.*

- The teacher will want to listen to the students tell their stories to each other. Pay special attention to good narratives that some of the reluctant students have told.

- **Say:** *While listening to the partners, I heard (name) tell a very interesting personal narrative. (Name), will you share your personal narrative with the class?*

- **Ask:** *As we were working on our anchor chart, what did you do today that made you more aware of what it means to be a good listener? How will you improve? Is there anything you would like to add to our chart?*

- Dismiss class practicing signals and behavior when returning to seats or moving on to write independently.

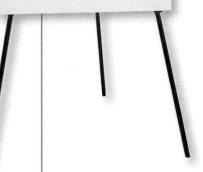

Characteristics of a Good Listener

1. Sit quietly.
2. Focus on the speaker.
3. Keep your hands to yourself.
4. Make mental notes.

DAY 4 – Preparing for Writer's Workshop
Creating a Topic List of Writing Ideas and Oral Language Development

Purpose

- Practice listening skills.
- Create a list of possible writing topics.
- Continue with oral language development.

Teaching Points

- Review and practice coming to the whole-group meeting area.

- **Say:** *Today I'd like to share another piece of narrative writing. This story is titled* **Wilfrid Gordon McDonald Partridge** *by Mem Fox (or* **All the Places to Love** *by Patricia MacLachlan). Please refer to our anchor chart to remind yourself about what it means to be a good listener.*

- Read the narrative to the students and model telling a personal narrative you have about any connection you can make to this book.

- Remind students of the procedures of turning and talking to a partner.

- **Say:** *Many of you have many stories you would like to share. Since I would like for each of you to have an opportunity to share your narratives, let's practice turning and talking to your partner.*

- The teacher will want to listen to the students tell their stories to one another. Pay special attention to good personal narratives that some of the reluctant students have told.

- **Say:** *While I was listening to (name's) personal narrative, it reminded me of another personal narrative that I have.*

- Tell the personal narrative to the students and then **say:** *I have told so many stories and I want to make a list of them. I will just write down a few words to help me remember the topic of my stories. For example, I just told you a personal narrative about (my grandmother's quilt). I will just write down "grandmother's quilt" on my list.*

- Model writing *I can write about . . .* at the top of a piece of chart paper. You will want to have a place to display this list when it is finished. Write a #1 and put "grandmother's quilt" after the number.

- **Say:** *Help me remember what some of my other stories were about.*

- As students brainstorm the stories that you told, list them on your chart.

- **Say:** *I loved telling these narratives, but I would like to tell the whole personal narrative in writing. You may want to write down some of your stories, too!*

- Dismiss class practicing signals and behavior when returning to seats or moving on to write independently.

I can write about . . .

1. grandmother's quilt
2. my pet's adventuresome day
3. my exciting weekend in . . .
4. spiders

DAY 5 – Preparing for Writer's Workshop
Creating a Topic List of Writing Ideas and Building Oral Language

Purpose

- Practice listening skills.
- Create a list of possible writing topics.
- Continue with oral language development.

Teaching Points

- Review and practice coming to the whole-group meeting area.

- **Say:** *Today I'd like to share another narrative. This narrative is titled* **Arthur Writes a Story** *by Marc Brown (or another narrative that centers around writing). Please refer to our anchor chart to remind yourself about what it means to be a good listener.*

- Read the story to the students and model telling a personal narrative you have about any connection you can make to the book.

- **Say:** *Many of you have many stories you would like to share. Since I would like for each of you to have an opportunity to share your stories, let's practice turning and talking to your partner.*

- The teacher will want to listen to the students tell their stories to one another and allow one or two students to share their stories with the whole group.

- **Say:** *All of you have shared many stories with your partner or with the class. Yesterday I made a list of the stories that I have told, and I would like you to be able to list your stories, too. Remember that you have told stories about memories, your family, animals, etc.* (Recap subjects that you have discussed.)

- Display the *I can write about . . .* list that you wrote during Day 4 and remind students how they helped you compile your list.

- **Say:** *Now think about all of the personal narratives that you have told during this week. We will now have time for you to compile a list of all of the narrative that you have told and any other topics that you might be able to tell.*

- Ask students to return to their seats to compose their lists. Support students who are struggling to remember some of the stories that they have told.

- After 10–15 minutes, use your signal to call students back to the whole-group meeting area. Ask them to bring their lists with them.

- **Say:** *You have each listed many of the narratives that you have told and other topics that you might be able to tell about. Some of you may not have finished your list, but you will have time tomorrow to add to it. Remember that this list will never be finished. You can always add to it whenever you remember something that you would like to tell or to write.*

- Dismiss students using your signal.

I can write about . . .

My best soccer game

Losing my best friend's pet

I can write about . . .

Snakes of the Amazon Region

Running a marathon

I can write about . . .

Shopping with my friends

My babysitting job on Halloween

Teacher's Note

For today's lesson only, the writing time is included in this lesson so that students will be prepared for Day 7.

DAY 6 – Writer's Workshop
Procedures: Using and Storing Writing Folders

Purpose

- Guide students in the proper use and care of their writing folders.
- Help students understand where their folders are stored and how to return them to the storage place.

Teaching Points

- Use your signal to call students to the whole-group meeting area.

- Hold up a folder that you have predetermined each student will use as their writing folder. (Usually these folders are uniform in appearance. They are the same color and type for easy identification as a writing folder.)

- **Say:** *You will each have a folder that looks like this. This is your writing folder. Please write your name on your folder (if it is not already labeled). You will use your folder to store all of your writing and other resources writers use. Your topic list will go inside this folder. When we come back for our mini-lesson, please bring your folder with you. We will store our folders (in a predetermined place) and return them when Writer's Workshop is over.*

- Emphasize to students that their folders should never go home and should not be kept in their desks. The folders will be needed for Writer's Workshop on a daily basis, and the folders must always be available.

- Model a folder you have assembled with your own writing. Show that your name is on the front of your folder and that you have included pieces of your writing that are "in progress" or "completed." You may want to show that you have stapled your topic sheet on the inside cover.

- **Say:** *Your writing folder is your tool to help you organize your writing and keep your writing from getting misplaced. It will be one of your most important resources when you write. You should keep it with you during Writer's Workshop.*

- **Say:** *We keep our writing folders in the same place each day. It is very important to get and return our folders carefully. We need to take good care of them because we will use them every day.* (Model the storage place and how the folders should look before and after the students have returned their folders to the proper place.)

- Distribute writing folders to students.

- If necessary, model for the students how to follow the procedure (calling rows, tables, students, etc.) when you are ready to end Writer's Workshop. Practice until the students are able to retrieve and store folders correctly and quietly.

- **Writing Time:** Distribute the topic list that they compiled on Day 5. Ask students to return to their seats. Invite them to place their name on the front of the folder and then add to their topic lists. Suggest that students who are ready might want to begin writing, and they may do so at this time. As students are working, circulate and help students staple their topic lists to their folders.

DAY 7 – Writer's Workshop
Choosing the Writing Topic

Purpose

• Guide students in the process of choosing a topic for writing from their list.

Teaching Points

• Use your signal to call students to the whole-group meeting area.

• The teacher should have his or her own topic list that was compiled with the students available to use for this mini-lesson.

• The students need to have their writing folder with them.

• **Say:** *These are all stories that I could tell and write. This one is one of my favorite topics. I will put a star beside this topic to remind me that I want to write about this topic first. Now look at your topic list. Decide on your favorite topic. Now turn to your partner and tell the whole personal narrative. Be sure not to leave out any details that are important to the narrative.*

• **Say:** *When you hear the signal, please take your writing folder and go back to your seat to write the entire personal narrative or all about the topic, exactly as you told it to your partner. If you don't finish, you will be able to continue with your writing tomorrow.*

• Distribute paper to the students.

• Dismiss students from the mini-lesson using your signal.

I can write about . . .

1. grandmother's quilt
2. my pet's adventuresome day
 3. my exciting weekend in . . .
4. spiders

DAY 8 – Concept of Writer's Workshop

Purpose

- Introduce concept of Writer's Workshop to students.
- Clarify the purpose of Writer's Workshop.

Teaching Points

- Use your signal to call students to the whole-group meeting area.

- **Say:** *Today we will be talking about Writer's Workshop and what it is.*

- Draw a blank three-column chart. As you explain and discuss the components (mini-lesson, independent writing time, and sharing time) of Writer's Workshop, you will complete the chart.

- Begin by explaining the mini-lesson. Write "Mini-Lesson" at the top of the first column.

- **Say:** *We have been learning about how we come together as a whole group to learn more about writing. This is one part of Writer's Workshop.*

- Write a few ideas in the Mini-Lesson column.

- Write "Writing Time" at the top of the second column. Explain that students will be doing different things during writing time. Explain that most of their writing time will be spent writing and using the writing process. Explain that the students will be learning about the writing process during their mini-lessons.

- **Say:** *After our mini-lesson, we will use what we learn about writing to write different pieces of writing that interests us. We will use the writing process when we write, so each of us may be at different places in the writing process.*

- Write a few ideas in the Writing Time column.

- Write "Sharing Time" at the top of the third column. Explain the students will have an opportunity to share what they have written with other students in the class. Explain that they will also hear what others have written.

- **Say:** *There will be times to share with the group or a partner about things you have written. You may get help from your friends about a writing problem, read an especially interesting part of your writing to a classmate, or listen to another student's writing as they read to you.*

- Write a few ideas in the Sharing Time column.

- Ask students to share ideas about how Writer's Workshop will help them become better writers.

- Dismiss students from the mini-lesson using your signal.

- Students will write independently at the end of each day's mini-lesson.

Writer's Workshop

Mini-Lesson	Writing Time	Sharing Time
1. Learn about writing.	1. Silent writing	1. Listen to other authors.
2. Examine other author's work.	2. Writing process steps	2. Read my writing.
3. Discuss how authors write.		3. Ask questions.

DAY 9 – Writer's Workshop Procedures
Using and Storing Writing Tools

Purpose

• Introduce students to storage places for writing tools.
• Guide students in the proper use and storage of materials.

Teaching Points

• Use your signal to call students to the whole-group meeting area.

• Tell your students that today you are going to tell them about a place in your room where they will find many things they will need as writers. Invite your class to come with you to the writing table or to the location in the classroom where materials will be stored. Tell your students that these are resources that they may need when writing, editing, revising, and publishing. (Have several different tools there to share with the students. Suggestions: loose leaf notebook paper, unlined paper, construction paper, stapler, tape, hole punch, rulers, scissors, pens for editing, sharpened pencils, markers, dictionaries, thesauri, etc.) Take the time to talk about each item, emphasizing that these are tools to use during Writer's Workshop only. Explain to students that it will be their responsibility to use the materials wisely and for the correct purpose.

• **Say:** *As we learn about the writing process during our mini-lessons, you will see how we use these tools.*

• Invite the students to return to the whole-group meeting area and find their seat. Debrief the location of the writing tools and their use. Create an anchor chart titled "Tools Students Use When Writing." Invite the students to help list the tools and note how each tool is used. Ask if they can think of other items that they might need during the workshop. Post the anchor chart over the writing table or in the writing area.

• Dismiss students from the mini-lesson using your signal.

• Students will write independently at the end of each day's mini-lesson.

Tools Students Use When Writing
1. notebook paper
2. unlined paper
3. pencils/pens
4. stapler

Looks Like	Sounds Like

DAY 10 – Writer's Workshop Procedures
Creating an Effective Atmosphere for Writers

Purpose

• Guide students in developing rules for Writer's Workshop.
• Help students understand what Writer's Workshop looks like and sounds like.

Teaching Points

• Call students to the whole-group meeting area using your practiced signal.

• Using the anchor charts, review with students what makes a good listener and what Writer's Workshop is.

• **Say:** *We know that during Writer's Workshop we learn about writing. There are ways that we can work together to make our classroom a place that will allow us to write well. Today we are going to brainstorm what we can do to make our classroom a place where we can write and collaborate.*

• Introduce a two-column T-Chart that will help students clarify what Writer's Workshop looks like and sounds like. Title the two columns "Looks Like" and "Sounds Like." This is a fluid chart that you will add to during the year as your Workshop develops.

• **Say:** *Close your eyes and visualize what you would see if you walked into our room during Writer's Workshop?* (i.e. students sitting on the floor in whole group for the mini-lesson, students talking with the teacher, students talking and writing with one another, students writing independently, students sharing, etc.)

• Record students' ideas on the T-Chart under the column "Looks Like."

• **Say:** *Now think what would you hear if you walked into our room during Writer's Workshop?* (i.e. students using tools, pencils scratching, students moving around the room quietly, students quietly sharing with partners and/or a teacher, the teacher teaching a mini-lesson, etc.)

• Record students' ideas on the T-Chart under the column "Sounds Like."

• Use the anchor charts as resources to revisit when you face problematic situations during your Workshop.

• Dismiss students from the mini-lesson using your signal.

• Students will write independently at the end of each day's mini-lesson.

DAY 11 – Writer's Workshop Procedures
Appropriate Behavior

Purpose

• Discuss behavior that is appropriate and conducive to writing.

Teaching Points

• Use your signal to call students to the whole-group meeting area.

• **Say:** *When I am writing, I need to be able to think about my good ideas and put those ideas in writing. I can't write well if someone is bothering me. What helps you to do your best thinking and writing? What helps Writer's Workshop run smoothly?*

• Brainstorm a list of appropriate behaviors and post them on a chart entitled "Writer's Workshop Rules." These rules could include:
—You may participate in the writing process during the entire time.
—You may not disturb others.
—You may sit in a comfortable place.
—Listen when asked.
—Be ready to share when asked.
—Make sure you get and replace your writing folder at the proper time, etc.

• **Say:** *I will place our rules on the wall so that we can refer to them at any time. In addition, if we think of other rules that we need to add, we can do that.*

• **Say:** *Be sure that you follow our workshop rules as you write today and every day.*

• Dismiss students using your signal.

Writer's Workshop Rules

• You may not disturb others.

• You may sit in a comfortable place.

• Listen when asked.

• Be ready to share when asked.

DAY 12 – Writer's Workshop
Procedures: Where to Sit

Purpose

- Guide students in sitting in the location that is most conducive to writing.
- Help students understand where and when they might move to a new location to write.

Teaching Points

- Use your signal to call students to the whole-group meeting area.

- Model sitting at your desk to write something.

- **Say:** *Is this the only place in the classroom that you have seen me write? What other places have you noticed me writing?*

- Brainstorm a list of places that students have seen you engaged in writing.

- **Say:** *You have noticed that there are many places in this classroom that I can write, and there are reasons why I might need to move to another location. As writers, you might be very comfortable writing at your desk, but there may be other places in this classroom that you might also be able to write. Let's create a chart to help us remember good places to write.*

- Create a web on chart paper that students can use as an anchor chart. Note any appropriate places that children might be able to sit during writing time (a table in the classroom, a corner that is away from others, a desk beside another student while conferring, on the floor, etc.).

- **Say:** *You can move to any place in the classroom that is comfortable and helps you to stay focused while you are writing. Remember that this must be a place where you are not disturbing others while they are writing.*

- **Say:** *Now let's practice finding a good place to write as we continue with Writer's Workshop.*

- Dismiss students using your signal.

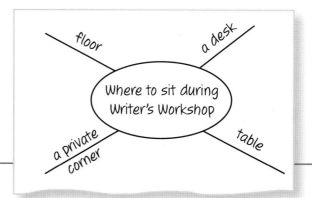

DAY 13 – Introduce the Writing Process

Purpose

• Review the prewriting piece of Writer's Workshop.
• Create an anchor chart with the writing process cycle.

Teaching Points

• Call students to the whole-group meeting area using your practiced signal.

• **Say:** *Today we're going to begin learning about the process good writers use when they are writing a personal narrative or any piece of writing. Most authors follow this cycle or one very similar to it every time they create a piece of writing. Since we're authors too, we want to learn how this cycle, or writing process, will help us be better writers. We have been writing stories and placing them in our writing folders. Now we will learn what we can do next.*

• Show students the list of stories that you made on Day 5. Add another topic to your list that concerns something that happened at school. The narrative writing should be one that students can contribute thoughts and ideas. Tell them that tomorrow they will help you write that story.

• **Say:** *Be thinking about ideas for the writing that we will do tomorrow.*

• Dismiss class from the mini-lesson using practiced signals and behavior.

• Students will write independently at the end of each day's mini-lesson.

Teacher's Note

It will be important to post a visual that will help students reflect on the writing process. The visual should be in a spot in the room that is accessible and continuously available for reference. (See figure below for a suggested format.)

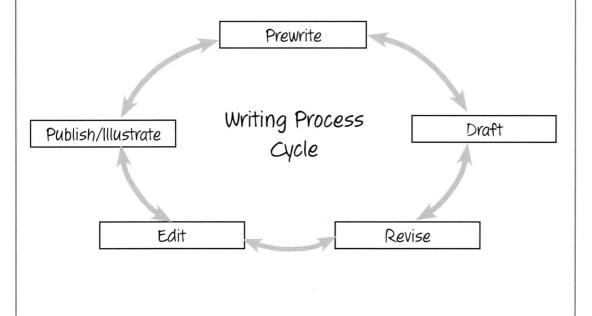

Teacher's Note

This is an excellent opportunity to begin creating a risk-free atmosphere in your room by accepting all ideas and allowing students to decide the direction of the narrative writing.

Remember

Make it clear to students that this is a short story that will be used to model the writing process. Too many details may create narrative writing that will be lengthy and hard to use for modeling purposes.

DAY 14 – Continue Prewriting Using a Web

Purpose

- Explain to students the importance of prewriting.
- Create a narrative writing web.

Teaching Points

- Call students to the whole-group meeting area using your practiced signal.

- Revisit the brainstorming process and remind students about the new idea that they will all help to write.

- **Say:** *When good writers begin a personal narrative or any writing, they use a tool to help them record their ideas so they can think about their narrative writing in an organized way. One of the tools some writers choose to use is a web. Today, we're going to use the idea we decided on yesterday to create a web for our narrative writing.*

- On a piece of chart paper, draw a circle in the center with the idea students chose to write about written in the center of the circle. Around that idea, write the details as students brainstorm creating a web that will drive the direction of the narrative writing. Be sure to guide students into including the literary elements of character, setting, problem, and solution. (See example below.)

- Dismiss class from the mini-lesson using practiced signals and behavior.

- Students will write independently at the end of each day's mini-lesson.

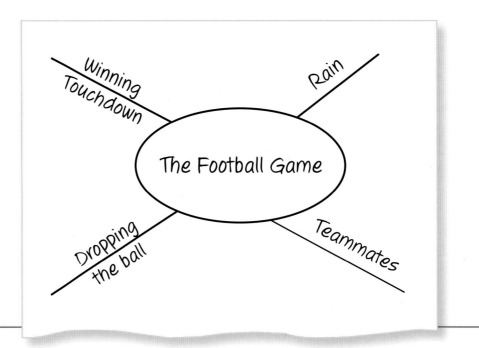

DAY 15 – Continue Prewriting

Purpose

• Create an anchor chart showing different kinds of prewriting.

Teaching Points

• Call students to the whole-group meeting area using your practiced signal.

• **Say:** *We have been using a web to do our prewriting for our narrative piece. As you practice writing, you may choose other ways to prewrite. Today we are going to create an anchor chart with different ideas about prewriting. The chart may help you choose a way to prewrite that will help you organize ideas for a piece of writing.*

• Using a piece of chart paper, title the anchor chart "Prewriting." Invite your students to give ideas of different ways to prewrite. (make lists, draw pictures, brainstorm, use graphic organizers, etc.)

• **Say:** *After you have finished your prewriting, remember to store that paper in your writing folders so you have it when you begin writing your narrative writing.*

• Dismiss class from the mini-lesson using practiced signals and behavior.

• Students will write independently at the end of each day's mini-lesson.

Prewriting

• Make lists.
• Draw pictures.
• Brainstorm.
• Use graphic organizers.

DAY 16 – Continue Prewriting

Purpose

- Review the prewriting step of the writing.
- Know that every piece of narrative writing has a beginning, middle, and end.
- Create an anchor chart showing the characteristics of a beginning, middle, and end of a piece of narrative writing.

Teaching Points

- Make sure you have the writing process anchor chart posted in a place where you can easily refer to the writing process cycle. Call attention to the writing process cycle and review the process of prewriting. Talk with your class about the next step in the process—rough draft.

- **Say:** *When a writer is ready to begin writing the rough draft, it is important to look over the prewriting and think about where to start writing. If a writer is composing a story, or a piece of narrative writing, it's important to remember that every narrative has a beginning. In the beginning, an author may reveal the character and setting.*

- Use the class prewriting from Day 13 and identify the character and setting.

- **Say:** *All narratives have a middle. In the middle, a writer tells about important details and events in the narrative writing. This may be a problem, a complication, a predicament, or an obstacle in the narrative writing.*

- Use the class prewriting to identify the points that may be in the middle of the narrative writing.

- **Say:** *Every piece of narrative writing has an ending. In the end, a writer could tell how a problem is solved.*

- Use the class prewriting to identify the points that could be in the ending of the narrative writing.

- **Say:** *When we begin our narrative writing, it will be important to use our prewriting to help us make sure we don't leave out any part of narrative writing.*

- Using chart paper, create a three-column T-Chart. Title the first column "Beginning," the second column "Middle," and the third column "End." Invite the class to contribute ideas of what a writer could put in the beginning of a piece of narrative writing (details describing a character[s], details describing the setting, etc.), in the middle (details describing a problem, events leading up to a problem, how a character reacts to the problem, etc.), and at the end of a narrative (details describing how a problem is solved, how a character feels about the solutions, how the solution affects the character, etc.).

- Post the anchor chart where students can use it for a reference to write the rough draft of the narrative writing.

- Dismiss class from the mini-lesson using practiced signals and behavior.

- Students will write independently at the end of each day's mini-lesson.

Beginning	Middle	End
Describe character	Describe problem	Describe solution
Describe setting	Events leading to a problem	Describe characters' feelings about solution

Teacher's Note

It's important to emphasize that, even though the rough draft is not the time to use a dictionary or look up words or ask how to spell words correctly, there are many words that the students do know how to spell. Your expectation is that these high-frequency words are not to be misspelled. Students will be at different developmental writing and spelling stages. A word wall is an important tool for students to reference at this time.

Day 17 – Begin Rough Draft Step of Writing Process Cycle

Purpose

- Review the Beginning, Middle, and End Anchor Chart.
- Understand that the rough draft is written on every other line.
- Begin writing the rough draft of your class narrative.

Teaching Points

- Call students to the whole-group meeting area using your practiced signal.

- It is important to have the writing process posted in a place where you can easily refer to the writing process cycle. Call attention to the writing process cycle and review the process of prewriting. Talk with the class about the next step in the process—rough draft.

- **Say:** *When a writer is ready to start writing a rough draft, the first thing that an author does is look at the prewriting to see where he or she wants to start. The last time we met, we identified the points that we could put at the beginning of our rough draft.*

- **Say:** *When an author is writing the rough draft, it is important that his or her attention is on putting thoughts on paper. You will probably make some spelling errors, grammar errors, or have story elements you will eventually want to change. The most important thing about a rough draft is that you spend your time writing and putting your ideas on paper.*

- **Say:** *It is also important to remember that we will write on every other line. Writers do this because there will come a time when they will need that extra line to fix up the writing.*

- Using a piece of chart paper, begin the process of writing the rough draft of your class narrative. (Be sure that you skip lines on the paper.) Invite the class to contribute ideas for the narrative writing using the prewriting web and chart as a guide.

- Begin writing the rough draft, inviting students to contribute sentences and ideas for the beginning of the class narrative. Continue with this process until your mini-lesson time is up. Tell the students that you will continue with the narrative writing tomorrow. You will use your mini-lesson time for the next couple of days until the rough draft for your narrative writing is complete.

- Dismiss class from the mini-lesson using practiced signals and behavior.

- Students will write independently at the end of each day's mini-lesson.

DAYS 18–19 – Continue Writing Process Cycle
Rough Draft

Purpose

- Continue using the writing process cycle (rough draft) to create a class narrative emphasizing a beginning, middle, and end to the piece of narrative writing.

Teaching Points

- Call students to the whole-group meeting area using your practiced signal.

- **Say:** *Today we will continue writing the rough draft of our piece of narrative writing. Who knows what part of our narrative writing we are ready to draft? How do you know?* (By looking at our prewriting and looking at the points we want to write about.)

- Reread the rough draft of what has been written so far. Continue writing the rough draft until your mini-lesson time is over.

- You will use your mini-lesson time for a couple of days to complete the rough draft.

- Dismiss class from the mini-lesson using practiced signals and behavior.

- Students will write independently at the end of each day's mini-lesson.

Teacher's Note

You will want to encourage your students to reread often. They need to make sure that their writing makes sense and that their message conveys what they intended.

DAY 20 – Completing the Rough Draft

Purpose

• Create an anchor chart entitled "Rough Draft."

Teaching Points

• Call students to the whole-group meeting area using your practiced signal.

• **Say:** *We have been writing the rough draft of our narrative writing. Let's create an anchor chart about the important points of a rough draft.*

• Using a piece of chart paper, title the anchor chart "Rough Draft." Invite the students to contribute ideas about writing a rough draft. (Write many sentences; follow your prewriting plan; write all of your narrative; make sure you write a beginning, middle, and end in your narrative; make sure you have characters, setting, problem and solution; correctly spell words that you know; put down what you know about words that you don't know, etc.)

• Post the rough draft anchor chart beside the prewriting anchor chart. This assures availability to the students when working their way through the writing process cycle.

• Dismiss class from the mini-lesson using practiced signals and behavior.

• Students will write independently at the end of each day's mini-lesson.

Rough Draft

• Write many sentences.

• Follow your prewriting plan.

• Write all of your narrative.

• Making sure you write a beginning, middle, and end in your narrative.

• Make sure you have characters, setting, problem and solution.

DAY 21 – Introduce Revising
Using a Caret

Purpose

- Introduce students to the revising step of the writing process cycle.
- Use completed class narrative to model revising concept.
- Model the use of a caret as a revision tool used to insert one or two words.

Teaching Points

- Call students to the whole-group meeting area using your practiced signal.

- **Say:** *Do you remember what a good reader does after they finish reading? That's right. They go back and think about their reading. A good writer does about the same thing. After an author has written the rough draft, a good writer goes back over their writing and thinks about how their writing sounds. There are many things to think about. An author may think about the character, setting, problem, and solution. They may think about using describing words, adding sentences to make their writing clearer, or adding whole chunks to a narrative to make it more exciting or easier for their audience to read. Today we're going to look at one way to revise your writing.*

- Reread the piece of narrative writing that the class wrote together. While you read, think aloud to model the process of adding adjectives to provide description.

- **Say:** *I'm reading this sentence. It says that . . .* (For example: "It says that the bear was chasing the rabbit into the forest. I ask myself what kind of bear it was. Was it a bear cub? Was it an enormous bear? How did it move? Was it hungry?") *I think that we could add words to this sentence to make it more interesting. We could also help the reader visualize the . . . What words do you think we could add to this sentence?*

- Continue through the writing finding appropriate places to use the caret. Then write an adjective above the caret on the blank line that is formed as lines are skipped during writing. Use some discretion when choosing words so that there are only a few examples.

- **Say:** *When you are ready to make revisions to your writing, you may want to try using a caret if you just need to add one or two words.*

- Dismiss class from the mini-lesson using practiced signals and behavior.

- Students will write independently at the end of each day's mini-lesson.

My teammate was

laying on the ∧cold ground

in the ∧pouring rain. I couldn't

believe I made that

kind of ∧horrible mistake.

p.3

DAY 22 – Continue Revising
Using Spider Legs

Purpose

• Model the use of a spider leg as a revision tool used when adding one or two sentences to a rough draft.

Teaching Points

• Call students to the whole-group meeting area using your practiced signal.

• **Say:** *The step of the writing process that we've been learning about is revising. This step is difficult for some writers because it's hard to change what they have written. Remember that, when we make revisions, we are making our writing more interesting, more accurate, and more complete. There are times when we revise that we may need to add more than a word to our writing. We many want to add a sentence. We're going to use a tool called a spider leg.*

• Read through the class narrative writing to find a place where another sentence could be added for clarity or detail.

• Model cutting a strip of writing paper and taping it on the draft where you want to add the sentence.

• **Say:** *Now you're ready to write your sentence(s) on this strip of paper. When you read the writing, read this sentence with the rest of your writing.*

• Continue modeling using the spider leg revision tool by inviting the class to find one or two different places where a sentence could be added to the rough draft that was written in class on Days 17–19.

• **Say:** *When you are ready to make revisions to your writing, you may want to try using this tool. The strips are already cut. You can find them back on the writing table* (or any place that would be convenient for students).

• Dismiss class from the mini-lesson using practiced signals and behavior.

• Students will write independently at the end of each day's mini-lesson.

I tackled the wrong

guy! I was so

embarrassed. that I wanted to run and hide

stunned
I looked at the ∧ faces

in the crowd. Then I looked at the coach.

*

p.4

DAY 23 – Continue Revising
Using an Asterisk

Purpose

• Model the use of an asterisk as a revision tool to add a paragraph to a rough draft.

Teaching Points

• Call students to the whole-group meeting area using your practiced signal.

• **Say:** *Sometimes when we revise our writing, we decide that we want to add a paragraph to our writing in order to make our writing more interesting or to help answer questions our audience may have about our writing. When we want to add several sentences to our writing, we use a revision tool called an asterisk. It looks like this: *.*

• Refer to the class narrative. Reread the class writing reading adjectives added by using a caret and sentences added by using a spider leg. After rereading, invite the class to contribute ideas about places where a paragraph or several sentences could be added to increase the readers' interest in the narrative writing.

• Decide with the class where the sentences need to be placed and what the sentences should say. Then, place an *1 where you want to make the revision. On separate sheet of chart paper, also place an *1 and write the paragraph. If there is another paragraph added, place an *2 where you want to make the revision. On the separate sheet of paper, add *2 and write the paragraph. Reread the writing after every revision to make sure it sounds correct.

• **Say:** *We have learned several ways to revise our writing. Today we will create an anchor chart entitled "Revising."*

• Invite the students to contribute ideas about revising and what methods they could use to revise. (Carets are used when adding one or two words; Spider Legs are used when adding sentences; Asterisks are used when adding paragraphs; Response groups are used to help an author revise, etc.)

• Post the anchor chart with the Prewrite and Rough Draft anchor charts. Remind the students to use these charts as a resource as they move through the writing process cycle.

• **Say:** *If you need to add many sentences to your writing when you make revisions, you may want to try using an asterisk.*

• Dismiss class from the mini-lesson using practiced signals and behavior.

• Students will write independently at the end of each day's mini-lesson.

> * We were taught at a young age to make sure we went after the right guys! How could I make this kind of mistake?

DAY 24 – Introduce Response Groups

Purpose

- Explain what a response group is.
- Model what a response group looks like and sounds like.
- Create an anchor chart about revision tools and how they're used.

Teaching Points

- Call students to the whole-group meeting area using your practiced signal.

- **Say:** *When you are ready to begin the revisions on your writing, it helps to have someone listen to your writing and give you ideas. Today we are going to use a response group to help us revise. A response group is a group of three sitting knee to knee and eye to eye. The purpose to give an author a place to read the writing and talk with an audience about the writing.*

- Invite a group of three students to sit on the floor in a triangle. They are close enough that a soft voice can be heard and used, but not close enough to touch. Inform the class that the person who asks for a response group is the author of a piece of writing. They then choose two people to join them in the group. Choose one of the group to act as the author. You may want that student to read a piece of their own writing or use the class writing.

- Model by having the author read the piece of writing and by having the other two students respond to the reading. Remind the students that respect and kindness are always used when participating in a response group. If students have difficulty with this, you might want to become one of the "students" in the group in order to model an appropriate response.

- **Say:** *You may want to call a response group when you are ready to revise. Only two response groups may be held at one time. This is the place where you may have your response groups.*

- Dismiss class from the mini-lesson using practiced signals and behavior.

- Students will write independently at the end of each day's mini-lesson.

Revising

1. Use carets for 1 or 2 words.

2. Use spider legs to add sentences.

3. Use asterisks to add paragraphs.

DAY 25 - Introduce Editing

Purpose

• Introduce students to editing.

Teaching Points

• Call students to the whole-group meeting area using your practiced signal.

• Point out the editing step in the writing process by referencing the writing process cycle.

• **Say:** *After authors have revised their writing, then they look at the next step in the writing process. This is the editing step. It is important that writing has no spelling, capitalization, or punctuation errors. The first step is for the author to look for mistakes by rereading. Then an author often asks someone to help them continue the process. You will do the same thing when you ask someone to be your editor. Your editor will help you read through your writing to look for errors. During the year, we will learn many new things about grammar, capitalization, punctuation, and spelling. You will be expected to use what we learn as you edit your own writing and the writing of others.*

• Edit your class writing or a story that has at least one spelling error, one capitalization error, and one punctuation error. Invite students to correct errors they see as you read the story.

• **Say:** *You may be ready to edit your writing. Remember to reread your writing to find and correct as many errors as possible before asking a classmate to be your editor.*

• Dismiss class from the mini-lesson using practiced signals and behavior.

• Students will write independently at the end of each day's mini-lesson.

Teacher's Note

Common editing marks are included on page 180. You will be the best judge as to the levels of mastery your students will have when identifying spelling, punctuation, and capitalization errors. You may want to create a chart for your students to use as a resource with the editing marks noted.

DAY 26 – Editing, continued

Purpose

- Explain that conferring with the teacher is part of the editing step of the writing process.
- Make an anchor chart about what to do as they wait to confer with the teacher.

Teaching Points

- Call students to the whole-group meeting area using your practiced signal.

- Point out the editing step in the writing process by referencing the writing process cycle.

- **Say:** *After authors have edited their writing with a partner, they are almost ready to publish their writing.*

- Display the story that was written together on Days 17–19 and reread it with students. Refer to the Writing Process Cycle chart.

- **Say:** *Now that we are almost ready to publish our writing, we need to confer with the teacher, who will be your editor-in-chief, the person in charge of publications. This is part of the editing process. I will be your editor-in-chief. When you get the editor-in-chief's approval, you may begin the publishing process.*

- Hold up a spiral or a loose-leaf notebook that is labeled "Conference with Teacher."

- **Say:** *You will sign your name in this notebook when you have revised, edited, and then reread your writing. When you sign, I may be busy working with other students, but this is your way of letting me know that you are almost ready to publish. I will get to you as soon as I can. In the meantime, you have choices about what you can do. You can begin to write something new. Since we know that Writer's Workshop is never finished, what other things could you do while you are waiting for a conference with me?*

- Create a web with "What to Do as I Wait for a Conference" in the center. Students might suggest: finish another piece of writing, edit with another student, be part of a response group, add to the topic list, prewrite, begin a new draft, etc.

- **Say:** *There may be other times during the writing process that you need to confer with the editor-in-chief. I want you to know that you are welcome to sign the notebook at any time—if you are stuck or if you need help in any way.*

- Refer again to the Writing Process Cycle. Make it clear to students that they must revise, edit, and reread before they are ready to confer.

Conference
with
Teacher

• Indicate where the notebook will be placed. It's a good idea to use yarn or a string to tie a pencil to the notebook.

• Dismiss class from the mini-lesson using practiced signals and behavior.

• Students will write independently at the end of each day's mini-lesson.

What to Do as I Wait for a Conference

• finish another piece of writing

• edit with another student

• be part of a response group

• add to the topic list

• prewrite

• begin a draft

etc.

Teacher's Note

Focus only on one or two teaching points. Keep in mind that the writing belongs to the student, and you are making suggestions for improvement. Always allow the student to make the changes on his or her own paper.

DAY 27 – Conferring with the Teacher

Purpose

• Discuss the procedures of teacher/student conferences and their importance.

Teaching Points

• Call students to the whole-group meeting area using your practiced signal.

• Point out the editing step with students and review with them what they need to do during this step of the writing process.

• **Say:** *After authors have edited their writing with their other writers, then they need to talk to the editor-in-chief. We will review your writing once again to ensure that it is ready for publication. We will read your piece together, and then we might focus on one, or possibly two, items that would improve your writing. You might choose to make any changes to your writing during the conference, or you might decide to go back to your writing place to do your final work. You need to have the approval of the editor-in-chief before you begin to publish.*

• **Say:** *Let's review the writing process. If we have revised and edited our writing, we are almost ready to publish. What should we do now? Yes, we sign the conference notebook so that we can meet with the editor-in-chief. When the teacher is ready to confer, we bring our writing folder and our pencil to the conference table. We are prepared to read our writing with the editor-in-chief.*

• Model the conferring process by selecting a student to sit with you and read his or her story. Tell something that you liked about the writing, and be supportive of the student's efforts. Then select one teaching point or suggestion for this student. Ask the student what he or she thinks about your suggestion, and ask if he or she would like to make that change.

• **Say:** *When you have revised, edited, and reread your paper, you are ready to confer with the editor-in-chief. Some of you might be ready for this part of the editing process.*

• Dismiss class from the mini-lesson using practiced signals and behavior.

• Students will write independently at the end of each day's mini-lesson.

DAY 28 – Publishing

Purpose

- Explain the publishing step of the writing process.

Teaching Points

- Call students to the whole-group meeting area using your practiced signal.

- Point out the publishing step in the writing process by referencing the writing process cycle.

- **Say:** *After authors have edited their writing, then they look at the next step in the writing process. This is the publishing step. As authors, we will decide on illustrations, charts, graphs, or diagrams that need to be added to the writing. In the publishing stage, we reread our writing to make sure the message says what we want it to say. We add any illustrations that are needed.*

- Display the story that was written together on Days 17–19 and reread it with students. Refer to the Writing Process Cycle chart.

- **Say:** *Now we are ready to publish our piece of writing. We can do this in many different ways. We are going to create an anchor chart to help us remember the many ways, and we may add to this chart when we think of more ways.*

- Brainstorm a list of final products, such as standard books, folder books, accordion books, flip books, shape books, posters, a script, newspaper or magazine articles, blogs, etc. If possible, show students examples of each of these types of publications.

- **Say:** *When you are ready, you can decide how your writing will be published and how it will be illustrated.*

- Dismiss class from the mini-lesson using practiced signals and behavior.

- Students will write independently at the end of each day's mini-lesson.

Teacher's Note:

You may want to decide if you want your students to rewrite their piece of writing in their best handwriting or if you want them to type it on the computer. If you are fortunate enough to have an assistant or a parent that can help with the word processing, that may be a way to expedite the publishing. Remember that published writing should be free of errors so that it can be read by others.

Ways to Publish

1. Standard books

2. Accordion books

3. Flip books

etc.

DAY 29 – Publishing, continued

Purpose

- Explain the publishing step of the writing process.
- Discuss text features that could be added to the writing during publication.

Teaching Points

- Call students to the whole-group meeting area using your practiced signal.

- Point out the publishing step in the writing process by referencing the writing process cycle.

- **Say:** *In the publishing stage, we reread our writing to make sure the message says what we want it to say. Then we add any illustrations, charts, or diagrams that are needed. We think about the cover and other features, such as a title page.*

- Display one or more books and point out the importance of a eye-catching cover. Show students the title page and explain why most books contain this page. Then read or thumb through the book to observe the value of the illustrations that are in the book.

- **Say:** *Let's look at the piece of writing that we wrote together. What should be on the cover? What would be on the title page? What illustrations would this book need?*

- **Say:** *When you are ready to publish, decide what features you will include in your book.*

- Dismiss class from the mini-lesson using practiced signals and behavior.

- Students will write independently at the end of each day's mini-lesson.

DAY 30 – Sharing

Purpose

- Explain the sharing step of the writing process.
- Learn appropriate responses.
- Understand the importance of the author's chair.

Teaching Points

- Call students to the whole-group meeting area using your practiced signal.

- Point out the sharing step in the writing process by referencing the writing process cycle.

- **Say:** *After authors have their writing published, they often like to share their writing with others. This is the sharing step. Authors are proud of what they have written.*

- Display the narrative that you have written.

- **Say:** *Now I am ready to share my personal narrative. I will sit in the author's chair, and I expect that you will listen carefully to my personal narrative. After I read it, I will ask if anyone has questions or comments about my personal narrative. You must be a good listener in order to respond appropriately. Let's think of questions or comments that would be appropriate.*

- Make a two-column chart. One column will be "Good Questions" and the other will be "Appropriate Comments." Brainstorm a list of questions and comments, and post it close to the author's chair. Remind students that they can add more to this anchor chart as they think of other questions and comments.

- While sitting in the author's chair, read the piece of writing to the students. Guide them to respond appropriately.

- **Say:** *When you are ready to share your writing, the author's chair will be ready for you.*

- Dismiss class from the mini-lesson using practiced signals and behavior.

- Students will write independently at the end of each day's mini-lesson.

Teacher's Note

You may want to do this lesson now so that students will know what to expect, or you may want to wait until a student is almost ready to share. It is helpful to have one of your own stories that you have published.

Appendix

Additional Mini-Lesson Suggestions

Procedural Mini-Lessons

- Structuring and sequencing, writing while conferring, and sharing
- Using materials, such as a stapler, staple remover, or hole punch
- Using a Writer's Notebook or writing portfolio
- Writing a heading
- Writing only on one side of the paper so that revision is easier
- What to do if you can't choose a topic
- What to do if you don't know how to spell a word
- How to work in ways which are respectful to other writers
- How to conduct a peer conference
- How to provide appropriate feedback
- How to use the revision checklist
- How to use the editing checklist
- Options for publishing
- Illustrating a published book

Craft Mini-Lessons

- Noticing the world through sketching, list-making, and note-taking
- Getting beyond "I like" and "I love" stories
- Writing based on one interesting idea rather than several less significant ones
- Choosing topics
- Telling life stories that others can relate to
- Writing in a variety of genres
- Writing for a variety of audiences
- "Showing" rather than "telling"
- Describing people
- Omitting unnecessary words, such as **and**, **then**, or **very**
- Writing with voice
- Writing effective leads
- Writing effective endings
- Connecting a lead and an ending
- Writing effective titles
- Adding information to improve clarity
- Deleting information for clarity and conciseness
- Enhancing meaning through illustrations

Convention Mini-Lessons

- Managing space on the page
- Using left-to-right and top-to-bottom progression
- Inserting spaces between words
- Using capital letters to start sentences
- Using periods to end sentences
- Differentiating between complete and incomplete sentences
- Using capital letters for proper nouns
- Using exclamation points
- Using question marks
- Inserting quotation marks
- Using commas to separate items in a series
- Using -ing endings
- Using -ed endings
- Using contractions
- Spelling (according to grade level)
- Parts of a letter
- Punctuating a letter
- Using picture dictionaries

Individual Writing Self-Assessment Checklist

Name: _____   Date Started: _____

Title: _____   Date Completed: _____

Directions: Check your work using the list below. Use the list to edit and revise your work.

My paper has a clear purpose:

❏ I stayed on topic.

❏ I supported my topic with at least two or three details.

My paper follows conventions:

❏ I used correct spelling.

❏ I used correct capitalization.

❏ I used correct punctuation.

❏ I used correct subject/verb agreement.

❏ I used correct sentence structure (no run-ons, sentence fragments, or confusing sentences)

❏ I combined short, choppy sentences to make them sound better.

My paper shows attention to the writer's craft:

❏ I started the piece with a strong lead to catch my readers' attention.

❏ I wrote an ending that tells the important information.

❏ I chose words that are strong, descriptive, and interesting.

❏ I did not use the same words again and again.

Editing Marks

Mark	What it means	How to use it
ℯ⁄	Delete. Take something out here.	We went to t̶o̶ the store.
∧	Change or insert letter or word.	San Francico, Calafornia my home.
#	Add a space here.	My family loves to watch baseball.
⌒	Remove space.	We saw the sail boat streak by.
ℯ⁄	Delete and close the space.	I gave the man my monney.
¶	Begin a new paragraph here.	"How are you?" I asked. "Great," said Jack.
⌐⌐	No new paragraph. Keep sentences together.	The other team arrived at one. The game started at once.
∾	Transpose (switch) the letters or words.	Thier friends with gifts came.
≡	Make this a capital letter.	mrs. smith
/	Make this a lowercase letter.	My Sister went to the City.
⊙	Spell it out.	Mr. García has 3 cats.
⊙	Insert a period.	We ran home There was no time to spare
⋏	Insert a comma.	We flew to Washington D.C.
⌄	Insert an apostrophe.	Matts hat looks just like Johns.
⌄⌄	Insert quotation marks.	Hurry! said Brett.
?	Is this correct? Check it.	The Civil War ended in 1875. ?
STET	Ignore the edits. Leave as is.	Her hair was brown. STET